To Play for Love

Lorelei Henderson

To Play for Love
Copyright © 2024 Lorelei Henderson
All rights reserved.

ISBN: (ebook) 978-1-958136-86-7
(print) 978-1-958136-95-9

Inkspell Publishing
207 Moonglow Circle #101
Murrells Inlet, SC 29576

Edited By Yezanira Venecia
Cover art By Emily's World By Design

DEDICATION

To my family, friends and most of all, my sons Amaru and Samir, I love you both beyond measure.

For Nelsan Ellis; cousin, we miss you and love you.

CHAPTER ONE

The scary thing howled in fury as it lunged around the corner, its razor-sharp claws swiping the air as it reached for its next victim. The people in its way screamed in terror and began running through the tall grass as fast as they could, with those who fell helped up by the others as they fled the chasing, clawing nightmare.

"Cut," the director yelled. Then, "Cut," again came from the second unit director as everyone froze. For good measure, another, "Cut," came from an assistant, which made everyone stare her way, causing her to turn a fiery red with embarrassment.

Okay, so not a big budget movie, Cassandra Chaletain thought as she stood with the other six extras. *No, we're background artist*, she reminded herself.

"All right, you got ten minutes," the second unit director yelled. "I mean ten, not twenty or twenty-two. Ten."

Some of the others moved toward the only bathroom or "honey wagon" as it was called—the worse misnomer Cassandra had ever heard. While a couple of the other background artists went for the craft table, which was half-filled with bottles of water, packaged sandwiches, energy bars, and a bowl of oranges, Cassandra walked over to the person who'd boxed the phones and retrieved hers. She saw there wasn't anything from Marty, her agent, not even a brief message from his assistant. *What's going on*, she wondered. If she'd gotten the part in the Taraj P. Henson movie, she should have heard by now. Not knowing either way was roiling her insides.

As she grabbed a much-needed bottle of water, the scary monster thing walked up to her and removed his all-encompassing head mask, revealing his bushy red hair tied in a ponytail and a grinning face.

"Thanks for the audition material, Cassie. I got the gig."

"Congratulations, Robert," she said, feeling genuinely happy for him as he put his clawed arms around her and gave her a hug. "I'm thrilled for you."

"I'm thrilled for me too," he said. "See you in the next scene."

Good for him, Cassandra thought, knowing how badly he'd wanted that part in the Tom Hanks movie. She opened the water and gulped it down. They'd been doing the same running scene for the last four hours, and she was parched. She finished her drink and thought about getting another when someone lightly touched her shoulder. She turned and saw it was her friend Sophia; they had known each other for years and had been working together for the last three weeks.

"This is my last day here," Sophia began excitedly. "I got the role of Francesca in Netflix's *The Hero's Next Door*, and I owe it all to that vignette you wrote for me." She threw her arms around Cassandra. "I can't thank you enough."

"You're so welcome," Cassandra said, glad for her friend, yet taken aback that Robert and now Sophia had gotten parts in major movie productions. "Robert just got a great gig too."

"I know, isn't it amazing?" Sophia said. "And it's all because of you." Her face glowed with happiness and immense possibility. "I read the vignette at the audition and did exactly like you told me—to go in there and speak the lines with purpose and heart, and I did it! Every word came out smoothly and joyfully, Cassandra. Your words gave me such confidence, I was able to show them what I was made of; what I could do if given the chance." She laughed. "And I got the part!"

"Two minutes," a loud voice called. "Then background action."

"Time for more green screen," Sophia said. "See you back there."

Cassandra looked after her friend for a long moment, a frown on her face as she placed the empty bottle in the recycle bin. Robert and Sophia had gotten work on feature films while she was still waiting to hear about her chance, even as that old saying flashed in her mind: no news is good news. Though in the entertainment business, it usually meant nothing good is coming your way if you don't go after it. She took out her phone and dialed her agent's number.

After two rings it was answered by his executive assistant, Aimee. "Hello, Cassandra. Marty's not here right now—he's meeting with the people from Paramount, and those meetings always take all day."

"Can you have him call me back as soon as he can, please?" Cassandra knew better than to ask Aimee for any information; the woman was the utmost in discretion. "No, never mind, don't worry about a callback," she suddenly decided. "We'll be done for the day soon, and I'll come to the office."

"All right, but I can't guarantee he'll be back even then."

"It's okay, I'll wait."

She hung up and with the frown still on her face, walked over to the tech-wrangler, handed her phone, and went back to work.

When Cassandra left the set, that tight feeling of restlessness and dissatisfaction that had weighed on her mind had grown. She drove directly to her agent's office located in the High Gate building in Center City. She anxiously took the elevator up to the top floor where Tommy Maxwell and Marty Sadler Agency was housed. The company was a mid-level talent outfit that she'd been with since she'd come to Hollywood eight months out of high school, having spent those previous months working in Filene's Basement to finance her trip West. That had been fourteen years ago, and in this world, it was a lifetime ago.

Cassandra entered Marty's semi-luxurious office suite where Aimee, who looked like a starlet herself, with her dark hair and flawless skin a-la-Kate Beckinsale, sat at a glass-topped desk. She was closely studying whatever was on the two screens on the desktop, typing a staccato rapid pace on the keyboard in front of her as she listened to whatever was coming out of the earpiece in one ear. When she saw Cassandra, she quickly got to her feet.

"Good, you're right on time. He'll be back in ten minutes; then he'll only have five minutes—literally—to speak with you, Cassandra. The Paramount folks will be coming back from dinner soon, and he can't keep them waiting." She walked over to a set of double doors. "You'll be more comfortable in his office."

Cassandra walked through to Marty's inner sanctum and took a seat at his round table, which was topped high with movie and television scripts. She sat for a few minutes looking out his office windows at the expansive view of Los Angeles, before reaching into her purse and taking out a notebook and pen. For as long as she could remember, she'd written short stories, even shorter word plays, small vignettes—whatever came to mind to past the time. Now, though, she was too nervous to think of anything to write, and returned the things to her bag.

The door opened and Marty hurried in. "Cassandra," he said and took both her hands in his, giving them a quick squeeze. He was a few inches shorter than she was, was totally bald, and had one of the most beautiful smiles she'd ever seen. "Did Aimee tell you?"

"I know, five minutes."

"Yes, so to get right to it—you didn't get the part, Cassandra."

For a moment she was speechless, then, "Why not? I

know I aced those four auditions." She tried to sound brave, even as she felt shocked disbelief and hurt disappointment at not getting the gig. She knew she shouldn't internalize this intense feeling of failure; she'd gone out for too many parts in the past and hadn't gotten them. Yet this one had been different; she'd really wanted it and had tried hard to come up with great lines, had come to each audition with new material so not to sound stale, and had read each part with fervor and heart. Still she had come up short.

"They went with someone with more experience and more previous speaking parts, and you don't have many."

"Not from lack of trying, Marty. I do everything I can to make every interview, never getting to a set late, never making any demands."

"I know." Marty nodded in agreement. "You did nothing wrong; it just wasn't meant to be. It's no doubt you had your heart set on the Henson movie, but it was out of your control, Cassandra. I'm on the look-out for anything that might be perfect for you. I promise. We'll see what happens with the next tryout."

"You said this would be perfect for me, and I didn't get it."

"Next time," he said softly.

"And the next and the next," she said tiredly—suddenly tired of it all.

They heard a commotion in the outer room, whispering and talking, and Marty said, "I have to finish the meeting."

"I have to go anyway."

She turned and walked toward the door.

"Something great will happen for you, Cassandra."

"Not unless I make it happen for myself," she said over her shoulder and exited the offices, not bothering to speak to the Paramount executives who were there to boost someone else's career, definitely not hers.

CHAPTER TWO

When Cassandra arrived home, she saw who was waiting for her and realized she'd forgotten all about their date. She sat in her car gathering herself, readying to act all that she was worth to get through the rest of this evening. After getting out of her car and locking it up, she walked over to where Josh Redmon stood leaning against his black Tesla S Plaid, smiling at something on his phone. He looked as if he hadn't a care in the world, which he didn't, she mussed as he bent and kissed her cheek.

"How was running through all that pretend grass?" he asked, opening his car's passenger door for her. He was a medium-height man with Brad Pitt blond good-looks he cultivated by wearing his hair shoulder-length.

"Okay, another day or two of shooting to go," Cassandra said and settled onto the butter-soft car seat, the air-conditioning a welcome respite.

"I don't understand why they can't just CGI you all in, Cassie—you're already extras," he said as he powered on the car with a touch of a button, which started with a whisper. "It's how they add everything anyway."

"I'm a background artist," she snapped.

"Uh-oh, you didn't get the part in that movie, did you?" She didn't answer, so he went on, "Don't worry, they probably would have CGI'd you in anyway." He laughed.

11

"If they did that, Josh, I would never have a job." Cassandra tried not to sound as annoyed as she felt at both him and his laughter. It was not a new feeling.

"You wouldn't need a job if you'd consider making us permanent," he said, taking an exit onto the highway. "You'll have all the free time in the world."

"This is what I do," she said shortly and stared out the window, not wanting to replay the same argument they'd been having for the last three months. Making us permanent, for Josh, didn't mean marriage but living together or, specifically, her giving up her apartment and moving into his house, a large four-bedroom, six-bath McMansion in a Calabasas gated community where people kept to themselves and wondered about how much money they had.

The thought crossed her mind—and not for the first time—that if she loved him enough, she'd do it. *Why was she questioning this—them—now*, she wondered? The only answer was that maybe it was another unsettling problem she was adding to her list.

"We don't have to go out to dinner," she said, suddenly feeling in need of some "alone time." "I can grab an early night instead, make something at home; that'll suit me fine."

"No, I promised you dinner," he said. "As a matter of fact, you mind going up the Coast to Malibu with me?"

"Josh, I'm too tired. Exhausted, actually, and only want a quick meal, then off to bed." *Definitely alone*, she ended silently.

"It won't take long, no kidding." He flashed her his best professionally whitened smile. "A quick meet with Ray King—I told you about him, right?"

"The real estate king up the coast."

"Right, and he promised us dinner, and you get to see his house; I told you about that too. Come on, Cassie, it'll be a nice diversion from your day."

"All right," she said, reluctantly giving in. "But not too long—I have an early call in the morning."

She startled as her phone pinged and quickly plucked it out of her bag, almost fumbling it out of her grasp at her eagerness. She felt a quick stab of disappointment at immediately recognizing the caller. It wasn't Marty with a new movie at Paramount but a video from her older sister, Talia. Cassandra tapped it and immediately started laughing as the image of her niece and nephew, Lexxie and Nicholas, appeared beside her sister. They raced small, brightly colored construction cars and trucks along the floor. Each tiny vehicle had a Cavil Construction logo, the company her father had worked for more than forty-eight years.

"Aren't they cute?" Talia's tinny voice came through as she held up a red, miniature dump truck to the screen. "They're going to be placed on every table as trinkets to take home. While you, sis, will miss out on the party, seeing everyone, and all the fun."

Cassandra held the phone up to Josh, who glanced at it briefly before his eyes went back to the road.

"My father drove these things for years. He could drive any construction vehicle ever made: scrapers, road rollers, excavators."

"Whatever those are," Josh said and pressed on the gas, allowing the car to eat up the road to Malibu.

"I'm sorry I'll miss the party too," Cassandra told her sister.

"You should be," Talia said, "everyone's going to be there except you—his famous daughter."

"I'm not famous; I'm a struggling actor like just about everybody else in this town."

"Well, to hear him tell it, it's only a matter of time before you get your first Oscar and a BET award."

The sisters laughed.

"Dad's always been my best cheerleader."

In the phone's background, she heard her niece and nephew squabbling and knew they were getting restless.

"The kids are tired of playing cars. Bye you guys," she called into the phone, then to her sister, "Video as much of the party as you can, be sure to catch Dad's embarrassment-mingled-with-shocked surprise at being thrown an elaborate retirement party."

"Will do, miss you, sis."

"Me too, bye."

Cassandra clicked off and stared out at the passing scenery. She did miss her family; they were so many miles away, and at this minute, this missing felt like an actual, physical ache in her chest. It also suddenly made her feel lonely and alone and searching, especially for an answer to the one question: Was it worth it? This acting thing? Well, that was two questions, she almost chuckled at that, yet it didn't make her feel any better.

CHAPTER THREE

They arrived more than two hours later at the front of an elaborate, black-gated community called Windswept Colony. There was a booth on one side of the road with a guard, who exited and approached the car with an iPad in one hand. Josh rolled down the window and gave the man his information. The guard tapped the screen and the gates parted quickly and silently. The King knew Josh wouldn't dare blow off his invitation, Cassandra surmised as they went through, the gate automatically closing behind them. She sat forward in anticipation of seeing grandiose house Josh had told her all about for the first time.

The driveway up to the Kings' home was palm-lined, long and windy, and took at least ten minutes to travel. Yet what waited at the end, Cassandra saw was well worth it. The place was magnificent, all light and glass. A man stood waiting at the top of the stone steps to greet them.

As they excited the car, the sound and smell of the ocean hit Cassandra first as the man walked down to them and outstretched a hand to Josh, who took it. The man was whip-cord lean, broad-shouldered, and looked as if he spent all his time working in the sun, though Cassandra suspected his deep tan came from hours on the tennis and golf course.

"Glad you could make it," the man said.

"Of course, Ray; I wouldn't have missed this for the world." Josh turned to Cassie. "Neither would have

Cassandra."

The man came around to her. "Well"—he took her hands in his, a small welcoming smile on his solid face— "Josh has told me how lovely you are, an apparent understatement." He turned to Josh. "Come on, you two, let's go in and see the real deal."

He led them up the stairs, letting them precede him through a set of blonde-wood double doors into a white, open-planned foyer. The inside view was laid at their feet, the darkening blue-sea spectacularly panoramic through clear, floor-to-ceiling invisible glass panels that swept the entire house from one end to the other. Cassandra felt as if she could reach out and touch the ocean and sky.

"I hope everyone's hungry," a quiet voice with a raspy timber said from behind them.

She turned as a woman glided down the expansive walkway that fronted the view. Cassandra decided she was around her own age, but that was where the resemblance ended. This woman, who clearly spent much of her time on her physical well-being, was groomed from the top of her auburn-colored hair to her Louis Vuitton slippers—a mogul's wife without a doubt, Cassandra saw.

The woman held out a well-manicured hand and smiled with perfect teeth and sky-blue eyes, her porcelain skin taunt and unlined. "Hi, I'm Pammie. Welcome to our home."

"Nice to meet you too, I'm Cassandra," she said to the woman dressed as if for a night out in full makeup and in a vintage leopard-spotted caftan. Cassandra turned toward the view of the vast, darkened ocean. "This is lovely. I would never get anything done; I'd stay planted at the glass looking out every minute."

"We rarely go out," Pammie said. "Don't need to with what we have outside our windows, nothing compares to it. Dinner's ready, but come on, I'll show you around before we eat and while those two"—she gestured briskly toward Ray and Josh, who had seated themselves in deeply cushioned chairs and were talking in lowered voices—"talk shop."

The large house was a series of open rooms with expensive furnishings, all of it dwarfed by the ocean view. There was one room though that caught Cassandra's curiosity; it was filled with tons of yoga equipment and clothing, mats, bolsters, socks, massage balls, sports bras and pants, blocks, and other stuff she couldn't imagine how to use or wear.

Once seated at the long dining table for dinner—where Cassandra sat opposite Josh in order to look out at the view—Ray kept up a stream of conversation over the meal of lemon chicken and spinach artichokes. He expounded on the state's current real estate market, the state's determination to build affordable housing when people who wanted—and could afford—palatial homes were left out of the discussion, and how state taxes were out of control. Josh hung on to the man's every word, seeming to agree robotically with Ray's every pronouncement.

Fed up with the domineering and short-sighted conversation, Cassandra broke in and addressed their hostess, "Did you decorate the house yourself, Pammie?"

Pammie shook her head. "Ray's first wife's work."

"Are you a yoga instructor? You seem to have all the needed equipment to teach any kind of class."

Pammie shook her auburn head again. "I was a commercial model—"

"Before I took her away from hawking bathmats and office supplies," her husband cut in.

"I was thinking about opening up my own yoga apparel shop," Pammie said, dismissing her husband.

"You seem to have all the equipment to go ahead right away," Cassandra said.

"Saying is not doing," Ray cut back in. "Planning and executing takes work, time, and effort. Pammie can barely make her nail appointment without a reminder. It's the reason why that room is still filled to the ceiling. Anyway, Pammie doesn't need to do anything." He stared at

Cassandra pointedly. "She has this beautiful house, financial stability, and a partner who doesn't need her to be everything. Or even anything at all."

Cassandra looked at Pammie. "But what do you need and want?" she couldn't help asking.

The woman, to Cassandra's absolute shock, shrugged, then said, "I want whatever Ray wants."

The two women didn't address each other again until it was time to say goodbye.

On the ride home, Josh tried to interest Cassandra in talking about the beauty of the house and its view, but she wasn't having any of it; Pammie's response—that shrug—was the only thing on her mind … and the only thing she wanted to talk about.

"I felt like I was in some alternate universe." She turned to him. "Pammie's an exotic bird in a gilded cage, but one made of glass. How can she want to live like that, Josh? When there are so many possibilities out there—especially for someone in her position, with her privileges and advantages, not having to face the added barriers of discrimination and devaluation—yet she sits there without a clue. She's free to do what she wants, to have what she wants, to be whoever she wants to be despite her husband. Yet, she doesn't know what she wants—how can that be?"

"All right, Cassie," he tried to soothe her agitation with an empty platitude. "Some people just want to 'be,' and that's it." He shrugged. "While you want to be this great actor and barely think of anything else."

"It's not all right, not for her, and not for me."

"What does it have to do with you?"

"I've always, always known what I wanted, or so I thought. And to meet someone who can have whatever she wants, do whatever …" Cassandra broke off. "Stop the car right here," she said suddenly. "I want to walk, to think."

"About what?" Josh appeared confused, but he pressed

on the gas, sent the car into the empty space in front of her building, and turned it off before turning to her. "It's not Pammie's fault you didn't get the part in that movie."

"You're right, Josh, it's not her fault the way I'm feeling, it's mine, and I have to do something about it."

"Like what?" he asked warily.

She didn't say anything for a minute, then, "I'm leaving town," she said decisively.

He stared at her open-mouthed. "What about your current shoot?"

"They can get anybody to run through CGI-generated grass."

"Where are you going?" he asked, sounding shocked. "Can we go together?"

"No, Josh." Cassandra got out of the car, closing the door almost eagerly behind her. She looked down at him through the open window. "I've decided to go home for my father's retirement party. There, I'll decide if I truly know what I want and need. Until a couple of hours ago, I thought I did—but maybe not. So, I'm going back to Boston to figure out the rest of my life."

CHAPTER FOUR

Cassandra saw Talia first and thought, as she always did, how beautiful her older, half-sister was, with her almond brown skin and dark, sparkling eyes beneath her bouncy rows of thick dreadlocks. Talia rushed through the crowd there to meet the flight's passengers and threw her arms around her sister. Though they had different fathers, they were as close as any siblings could be. Cassandra returned the embrace just as tightly; happy to see her too.

"Sis, you stand out in a crowd," Talia said warmly. "It's wonderful that you're finally here." She pulled back and admired Cassandra's long, burnished hair, honey-colored skin kissed by the sun, and hazel eyes. "You look terrific."

"Sure, I do," Cassandra said, amused, "after a six-hour flight sitting between two guys—one who didn't believe in deodorant and the other a garlic lover—yuck" She suddenly grinned. "Great to see you too. Let's get outta here; I'd forgotten how busy Logan gets this time of year."

They walked quickly down the sliding walkway and out of the airport to the car park where Talia's beloved blue Subaru waited.

"I'd also forgotten how hot it gets in the summer—how humid," Cassandra said, and as soon as they settled in their seats, she turned the car's air conditioner to high.

"I have to make one stop before we go home," Talia said

and started the car, pulling out into the traffic headed into Boston.

"No problem, I appreciate you taking a break from work to pick me up, sis. How you like being back for good?" Cassandra asked, thinking her sister did look less stressed, more at ease since the last time she'd seen her a year ago in New York.

"Well …" Talia seemed to ruminate over the right words. "I find myself enthralled, captivated, spellbound."

"What?" Cassandra laughed. "By Boston? You're joking."

"By Roxbury, our old neighborhood and what it's become and becoming. Wait until you see it, Cassie. I've always thought of this town as full of working-class stiffs. Cold. Unfeeling—one of the reasons I took off for New York in the first place—but I was wrong. Let's take the long route to my place, through the Sumner across the Lenny so you can see the city approaching."

"Don't bother."

"Why not? You'll get to see some of this places' redeeming qualities for yourself."

Cassandra couldn't help but laugh derisively at her sister's statement, wondering what had come over her … and for Boston of all places. Yet, as they traveled toward home, she opened the window, laid her arms across the window seal, and watched the city grow toward her over the artistic Lenny Bridge, with its winged arches, through old world North End, and finally by the Charles River; it's presence eternal.

"Could it be, Talia"—Cassandra turned questioningly to her sister—"that now that you're at WHCK FM—"

"—WHCK, WHCK, WHCK," Talia broke into a chant of her radio station's call letters. "Wic-ked fun!"

"—as a station producer plus on-air-talent instead of an assistant like you were in New York has helped change your feelings about your hometown?"

"I thought that was it at first," her sister began, her tone serious, even pensive, "but then I got to talking to people in the community from Roxbury to West Roxbury and in between. To people whose families have been here forever or who just immigrated last week. The other day I spoke with a woman who'd only just arrived two days before from Trinidad; her first time in the U.S. She could have gone anywhere but chose Boston. She told me why she loved it here: her family who'd arrived here first, the diverse neighborhood she lived but with a flavor of home, the acceptance she'd found in her part of the city. It all made me realize those are the same reasons that pulled me back: our neighborhood being revitalized—it's history of Malcolm and Martin, folks embracing the crazy cold winters and scorching summers because they have to, who feel there is no place in the world they fit except for right here."

"So, you feel that way now? Despite the gigantic hurdle who is our mother—whom we love—and her die-hard attitudes, to put it bluntly."

Talia sighed dramatically as she wheeled the car expertly through the Indy-paced traffic. "There's nothing I can do about how she feels, and I'm tired of trying."

Not wanting to dig into a wound that seemed to have no hope of closing, Cassandra started to change the subject when her phone rang. She looked at it. "It's Mom." She grinned. "She must have heard us talking about her. Shh …" She hit the speaker button and answered. "Hi, Mom, how are you?"

"Fine, honey. Putting the finishing touches to Dad's show. I just saw the huge cake Layla ordered for him—his favorite, a cassata."

"He's going to love it."

"I'm so sorry you won't be here, Cassie," said their mother as her daughters glanced knowingly at each other. "We understand, you're working and the director can't afford to let you go right now."

"I'm sure he doesn't think that way, Mom."

"Be positive, daughter. Haven't I always told you—you

can do anything. You're talented and smart; you shine."

"Got it. Listen, Mom, I have to go. See you …" She clapped her hand quickly over her mouth as Talia looked over at her wide-eyed. "I mean, talk to you next week."

"Okay, soon, sweetie, and be careful, Cassie. Love you."

"Love you back." She clicked off.

"You almost gave the whole thing away," Talia admonished.

"I know," Cassandra said on a combination wail and giggle.

"Some actor you are."

They looked at each other and burst into peals of laughter.

As they headed into Roxbury proper and into Nubian Square, the heart of the neighborhood, Cassandra stared around at all the changes that had taken place since her last visit.

"Wow." She pointed at a beautifully constructed office building made of soft-reflecting glass of various colors that housed both a bookstore and a museum. "When did they build the Times Digital Center?"

"It opened six months ago and is rumored to be made of all sustainable materials."

Next to the center was a Hyatt Grand Hotel and plaza that swept at least two blocks and looked to house, not just the hotel but high-end shops as well.

"Wow," Cassandra said again, realizing the square had greatly evolved and was now a true center of commerce and entertainment, as vibrant and alive as any other grand city she'd ever visited.

"I have a quick meeting at the new Roxbury Theater." Talia turned the car down Silvan, one of the busier fairways lined with restaurants and shops.

"You sure Dad doesn't know I'm coming?" Cassandra asked again, wanting to be certain he had no clue and would be overwhelmingly surprised at her appearance.

Her sister shook her head. "Step-D believes you're

working on a movie just like Mom said."

"I wish you wouldn't call him that; it doesn't sound right."

"Only to your ears," Talia tossed back. "It's uber respectful and better than calling him my stepfather, or how about your-dad-not-mine? Better yet, my mother's husband."

"All right, all right, I get your—" Cassandra began and cut herself off in mid-sentence when she saw, in the middle of the block, the newly built Roxbury Theater with its distinct marquee and beautiful buildings that were so outstanding, it sat like a jewel on top of a crown. "It's wonderful," she said and meant it.

Talia drove the car around the gracious buildings so Cassandra could take it all in, then around back into a generous lot where a brand-new shuttle bus that featured the theater's name on its side was parked.

Talia slotted the car in among a host of work vehicles both women were familiar with as hard-hatted and Day-Glo vested workers moved in and out of the back carrying tools and construction materials.

"Dad told me they were building a movie theater," Cassandra said, "not a grand theater."

"It's that and more; it's a palace. There's staging for plays, of course, a movie house, an exhibition gallery, a student learning center, and even a restaurant café. I'm going to do a radio show from here at the premiere of a newly found play by the great Lorraine Hansberry. I'm here now to talk with the publicist and—if he's not too busy—the builder."

They exited the car trying their best to skirt the construction people coming back and forth. They had started up one of the bluestone pathways when Talia stopped and patted her pockets. "Hold a sec, I forgot my phone." She turned back and went the way they'd come.

Cassandra continued up the walk toward the double-glass entrance doors when she was suddenly bumped from behind. When she turned, a stack of wooden dining chairs were being held aloft by strong arms. Through the chair's slats, she caught a glimpse of bright gray eyes in a solidly handsome brown face partially covered in a neatly trimmed beard.

They stared at each other through the slats for brief, heart-pounding seconds with a sudden irretrievable fore knowledge of the past and the present entwining like lovers.

"Sorry," a deep, rum-colored voice said from the stack. "I wasn't paying enough attention to where I was going."

He side-stepped right at the same time Cassandra did, causing them to bump again before he pulled off a deft twist, turning the chairs from between them out of harm's way as he circled around her. He took a few steps, stopped a beat before moving off, and disappearing inside.

She stared after him. For a moment, she thought she'd recognized him. It was the voice … she knew it yet couldn't place it. Then again, it could just be her active imagination.

"What's wrong, Cass?" Her sister had come up beside her.

"I thought I recognized someone, but maybe not."

"Come on, I'm late." Talia hurried ahead of her. "Wait until you see the inside."

They entered through the glass double doors that were etched with the words *Welcome to the Roxbury Community Theater* in gold leaf lettering. Standing in the grand lobby on warm marble, Cassandra found herself awed by the palatal interior, its classical pillared beauty, the ornate walls covered in mosaic tiles up to its soaring ceilings. She couldn't believe such a place was right here in the heart of Roxbury.

To their right was a grand staircase covered in cranberry-colored carpeting while on the other side was a running up/down escalator. They took it up three floors to a set of office suites, and as they stepped off, a pretty young woman appeared out of one of the offices and walked toward them, a welcoming smile on her face.

She stopped a few steps away. "I was on my way down

to check if you'd arrived yet," she spoke to Talia.

Cassandra saw that she was more than pretty; she was out-right lovely. She was small, with long dark hair and skin the color of creamy, warm milk—a true Snow White with her black eyes and full lips colored ruby red. She and Talia looked at each other wordlessly for a heartbeat, then another long enough that Cassandra thought, *uhm?*

"Katelyn, this is my sister Cassandra," Talia introduced them. "I told you about her."

"It's nice to finally meet you," Katelyn put out a hand, and Cassandra returned the gesture. "When I watch a show, I try and see if I can catch you in there somewhere."

"You'd have to be really quick to catch a glimpse of me," Cassandra said.

"Didn't I tell you this place was incredible," Talia said enthusiastically.

Cassandra nodded, amused by her sister's enthusiasm she suspected had more to do with the pretty Katelyn than the building's attributes.

"It's more amazing than you can see from here," Katelyn added. Demarion Asher, the architect, did a wonderful job. Please take a tour if you want, starting down on the second floor and going up. I'll get you one of our informationals; it's pretty glossy and impressive if I say so myself. I'll be back in a minute." She turned and walked toward the offices.

"She created the brochures," Talia said, "and did a great job too."

"Did she?" Cassandra said and turned to her sister. "She seems nice and is definitely gorgeous. Are you and she …?"

"Don't go there, Cassie," Talia chided, recognizing her sister's tone. "We haven't been together long."

"Give it a chance then. You should ask her to Dad's party."

"Cut it out, Cass. Layla might not be too happy to see me show up with Katelyn, especially if Alex is not around."

Cassandra frowned at the comment. "Layla is our sister;

she would be happy you found someone. As for Alex and the claim he and Layla are partners? I'm not so sure about that; she spends more time taking care of the home and hearth while he's out doing whatever."

"I don't ask about what's going on with them—Layla and I aren't as close as you and me. Even though the three of us share the same mom, you two share a mom and a dad, which has always made me the odd one out. The different one."

"Then we're both different ones; me with my Hollywood aspirations."

Katelyn appeared again, putting an end to their conversation, and held out a large, glossy pamphlet that could have been a coffee-table book. Cassandra took it and flipped through it, noting how luxurious the theater was; its extravagance was equal to any of the world's most glorious venues.

"I'm going to look around," Cassandra said, eager to see more of the place on whom boards (in her active imagination) she would love to tread as Ruth Young from *A Raisin in the Sun* or Berniece Charles from *The Piano Lesson*, or even Juliet Capulet from *Romeo and Juliet*.

"Yes, why don't you," Talia seconded before looking at Katelyn. "I have the list of questions, not too long a list, but it'll take a few minutes to go over."

"We can do it in my office. I can show you the music setup for the opening while we're there."

The two moved off close together, laughing and talking in animated tones.

"Nice to meet you," Cassandra called after them, not at all put out when she didn't get a response.

CHAPTER FIVE

Doing as recommended, Cassandra took the escalator back down to the first level. She peaked into the main "house," at the descending rows of cushioned seats down to the huge stage below surrounded by technical sound and advanced lighting equipment she couldn't have named if she'd tried. The curtain was a golden fall and looked a mile high. There was a wide and generous orchestra pit. It thrilled her to know there would be an orchestra, with its violins, cellos, flutes and bass horns.

She took the magnificent staircase up to the second level, where a restaurant-avec-café that looked as if it had been moved whole from Paris or London, was in its final stage of completion. Workers were busy installing tan leather booths and small chandeliers overhead.

From a room off Cassandra's left, she heard the rum-colored voice again of the workman who'd done the chair-dance with her. She looked over as he appeared in the doorway, his back to her.

"Charlie, I want those Ruscha prints here tomorrow, pay extra if you have to; we can't have bare walls."

The man turned, and they locked eyes. Suddenly she recognized him.

Cassandra felt a frisson of electricity cross her nerve endings, making her supremely aware of the chance of their lives coming together so many years later. She and this man had once been friends in high school … no, more than friends, they'd hung out together, though never truly dated.

They'd liked each other tremendously until it had blossomed—at least on her part—into a sweet, young love; always there but never truly acknowledged by either one. There had been no one like Michael since. And because of time, circumstances—life—they'd lost each other until now.

"Michael Kiley, it is you, after all this time," Cassandra stated emphatically, studying the man, her eyes moving from his neatly cut black hair, work-tanned light skin, gray eyes, straight nose, and shapely defined lips within his dark beard. It was a while back, yet she could never forget the handsome face and tall, lean, muscular physique. "I'd know you anywhere." She grinned.

"Cassandra Chaletain." Michael smiled back in obvious delight. "It can't be you."

"Oh, yes, it can," she answered with a bit of her usual sauciness.

"Downstairs, I thought, *It's her*, but then, *No way would she be here—my heart's secret love that has grown all these years instead of diminished*. But here you are."

He reached out, she reached back, and they hugged briefly before pulling back and giving each other an up-close once-over.

"You look the same as you did throwing touchdown passes on the Roxbury High football field."

"Those touchdowns got me to Stanford, the rest I had to do on my own."

"And to end up back here, working construction. Is that what you do now?"

"Among other things," Michael said succinctly, then, "I've seen you in so many things: *The Have and Have Nots*, *Love Thy Neighbor*. The movies too: *San Andreas* and *C'mon, C'mon*."

"How could you have picked me out in that movie?" she asked astounded by his revelation. "There were a hundred people in that Venice Beach crowd scene."

"Easily. You were center right, walking next to a girl in sunglasses."

"I'm impressed," Cassandra said. "I don't think I could have picked me out."

"You always stand out, Cassie."

Cassandra stared at him. "Really? You're the only one from school I ever allowed to call me, Cassie."

He nodded, his gaze fixed on her face.

"It's crazy to see you after all these years," she said.

"You too, except for seeing you on the screen, of course."

"What else have you been up to? You were just as good at poetry and acting as running down a field."

"I was no actor, just good at painting scenery and carrying stuff from place to place."

"You were more than that," she said. "How long have you been working for the theater? How long back in Boston? I know I should keep up with our classmates on Twitter and Instagram, but then"—she shrugged—"I don't want to."

Michael laughed. "I probably should do better at keeping up too. How long are you going to be in town?"

"For just a few days. I'm here for my dad's retirement party."

"Michael," a man called from the other side of the restaurant. He had an accent Cassandra thought familiar.

"Uh-oh, I'm keeping you from your job. I hope your boss doesn't get angry at you."

"It's okay," Michael said.

A few seconds later, a white-haired man wearing a white summer suit followed the voice. He had the look of someone who frequented international fashion shows. "The menu is perfect," he addressed Michael, and Cassandra recognized his accent as distinctly French.

"It's great, Gaspard; except it doesn't have enough vegetarian dishes—two more of those I think, then it'll be perfect."

"Bien, Michael, I have just the two, and I have one recipe I tried out this morning. I will bring a sample for you and your friend to taste," Gaspard said.

"No, that's okay," Cassandra said, horrified. "I'm not here to make extra work for anyone."

"It's all right," Michael soothed. "It'll only take him a minute to prepare the dish. He pulled out a chair from one of the tables. "Please sit down a minute."

"I don't want to get you into trouble," Cassandra said and reluctantly took the seat.

Michael went around and sat across from her, looking at his watch.

"Break time is in fifteen minutes anyway; we're just a few minutes early, that's all."

Cassandra suddenly felt awkward. "I'm glad to see—"

"—It's great that—"

They spoke simultaneously, then halted, embarrassed. They turned as Gaspard appeared, holding up a tray in the air as if he was serving a supper for royalty.

"It is magnificent. I promise you will adore it."

He sat the food in front of them along with linen-wrapped utensils. On small plates were even smaller servings of what looked and smelled to Cassandra like meatloaf with a delicate sauce on top it; along with what looked like mashed potatoes, and a helping of sliced and glazed sweet potatoes.

"It is all plant-based with a mix of lentils and finished with a delicate sauce and glaze to highlight its luxurious taste and richness," Gaspard beamed.

Michael picked up his knife and fork. He shot a wink at Cassandra and began to eat.

Taking a deep breath, Cassandra forked a tiny piece of the meatloaf into her mouth, ready to swallow and smile even through the pain of bad food, but to her surprised delight, the meatloaf, or whatever it was, tasted absolutely delicious. It was light and wholesome and better than any meatloaf she'd ever had.

"It's delicious," she told Gaspard before trying some of the mash potatoes."

"The potatoes are really cauliflower. I add my own special cream and a few other touches to give them greatness."

"Gaspard, you've outdone yourself, as usual," Michael said. "All of it will be on the menu, is that right?"

"Of course," Gaspard said, and with a slight bow, left them alone.

They finished the small samples in record time, Cassandra enjoying the small meal as well as Michael's company.

"That was terrific," she said, taking a sip of the bottled water Michael had handed to her. "You have to stop giving me stuff. Your boss will have a fit at what you're doing. You might lose your job." Cassandra stepped away from him. "I'd better go." She moved toward the escalator.

"Take your time seeing the rest of the place," Michael said. "Go anywhere you like."

Talia suddenly bounded up the escalator, stopping next to them.

"I was looking for you everywhere," she said to Cassandra. "Did you know there's an art gallery featuring local artist's work on the third level?" She turned to Michael. "Mr. Kiley, your theater grows more terrific each time I visit."

"Hello, Talia. Again, please call me Michael. It's Roxbury's theater." He bowed slightly. "Thank you on its behalf."

"Your theater?" Cassandra stared at him open-mouthed. "You're not one of the workers then?"

"Worker?" Talia stared at her sister as if she'd lost a few brain cells. "He built this beautiful place and is responsible for the other projects in Roxbury. That's why I'm here— I'm going to interview Michael before the big opening."

"Why didn't you tell me?" Cassandra asked him, feeling

taken aback by the news, a flash of embarrassment heightening the color in her cheeks. "I thought you were a laborer or something."

"I'm a something." He grinned, his eyes taking her all in.

"You know my sister?" Talia asked.

"We were in the same class in high school."

"No way." Talia looked from one to the other. "A small world, right? I think I remember you; you were on the football team. You were one of our outstanding freshmen players—I don't know how I remember that, since I was a senior and had time for only one thing: graduating as fast as I could."

"No, it was two things," Cassandra corrected. "Getting out and how many hours you could DJ and party before passing out from exhaustion."

"Katelyn said your turntable skills were legendary," Michael said, "so I can't wait to hear what you bring to the opening."

"I got mad plans for that night, believe me."

Michael's gray-eyed gaze was pulled back to Cassandra. "You said only a couple of days?"

"At most." She stared back, feeling a shift in her world that for a brief moment, frightened her.

"Boss," a man in a hard hat and heavy work gloves called from the top of the escalator, "two of the plates around the boiler are cracked, and they were only put in yesterday. I pulled at one, and it came up easily."

"I'll check them," Michael said, his eyes never leaving Cassandra.

Talia checked her phone, then said, "We gotta go anyway to get ready for tonight."

"All right." Cassandra nodded at Michael. "Great to see you again."

"Same here."

They turned toward the escalator and took it down; Cassandra didn't look back, fighting every urge to do so.

CHAPTER SIX

Michael stood in his office on the building's top floor and watched out the window as Cassandra and Talia got into their car and drove away. Cassandra Chaletain right here, back in Boston; he could hardly believe it. His unrequited love. When he'd first seen her, he'd really thought it was his imagination. He'd thought about her often over the years. No, more than that, he'd actually seen her out at parties when he'd been working out in La-La Land. She'd always been on the arm of a guy who'd acted as if he owned the town.

The last time she'd been wearing a black-and-gold dress with her long burnished hair brushing her shoulders. She'd been part of an animated conversation with a group of dressed-to-the-nines party-goers, yet she'd stood out even among them. Everyone seemed to have been drawn to her, and he'd been no exception, even though he hadn't approached her. Cassandra was a talented, beautiful woman, and she was back. Now was his chance.

Michael picked up his pinging phone, read the message, and left the room. Outside, he walked down the side of the building until he came to an open space that was topped by concrete. His business partner and best friend, Demarion Asher, wearing a straw hat and rubber gum boots, lay on the ground tapping at the concrete with a finger.

"Why did I need to hurry down and watch you poke at the ground?" Michael asked in lieu of a greeting.

"Because it's wrong." Demarion got to his feet and threw out an impatient, expressive hand. "This is here for no reason at all."

Demarion was a slim, handsome man who'd been stopped countless times on the street by fans who confused him with the actor Brian White, who coincidentally was also from Boston.

Michael and Demarion had bonded at Stanford, both being from the same state and growing up in the same kind of neighborhood, though Demarion's had been Mission Hill. His parents were from Haiti, medical doctors who'd escaped the revenge of Jean Claude Duvalier. Demarion, an accomplished architect who'd planned the theater and the soon-to-be clinic, considered himself a gentleman farmer more than an accomplished building designer.

"We can't have this sort of thing; it's not right."

"Okay," Michael said, not yet getting what the fuss was all about. "How's your wife feeling?"

"Hannah's tired but happy. She can't wait for this baby to come. She says it's a boy by the way, and he's going to be early. I don't know how she knows these things"—he sounded mystified—"but she does."

"She should," Michael said drily, "with this being your fourth."

"And to think we were gonna stop at one." Demarion suddenly grinned. "How crazy was that? Our babies are amazing."

"Yes, they are," Michael agreed. He was godfather to their three—soon to be four—little ones and enjoyed it tremendously. "You still haven't told me why we're looking at the ground?"

"I did. I said it's not right, so I'm going to have this concrete removed and the space dug up."

"Why isn't it fine just the way it is?" Michael asked cautiously.

"Don't you see it?" Demarion gestured again at the uninspiring slab. "It's negative space. People don't walk it, they go around to avoid it because it's useless, unnecessary, and needs to be fixed. In its place, I'm going to plant grass, trees, and flowers. Eventually I'll put in benches so that in a few years people will have a place of beauty to sit, to contemplate and enjoy."

"You're right, Dee." Michael nodded, finally seeing what his friend was seeing. "It will be great green space; let's do it."

"Already underway. The digger will be here in the morning."

"Then, why'd you need to talk to me about it if you've already set up the project?"

"First of all, we're business partners"—Demarion faced Michael with an exacting tone—"and we consult each other on every component of our projects. Secondly, I saw the nice young woman from the radio station walking out and with her was someone else, also very pretty, and who I thought I recognized for some reason."

"That was *the* Cassandra Chaletain."

"Yeah?" Demarion took out his phone and held it up to Michael. "These are the trees we'll plant, Kousa dogwood." Michael nodded at the picture and before he could comment, Demarion leaned back and studied him. "Cassandra? You've mentioned a Cassandra—no, Cassie— to me a few times ... actually way more than a few times."

"That was her," Michael said shortly. "Listen, Dee, I'm going back in to finish some paperwork."

"Your Cassie?" Michael now had Demarion's full attention. "Here? She come back for a visit, or is she staying? She done with Hollywood too?" He was curious about the woman whom Michael had never forgotten. "Can't wait to meet her. Wait until I tell Hannah. Hey, we should all get together. When are you going to see her again?"

"Tonight, her father's retirement party."

"That's fast work on top of being a good thing. It's been too long since Christina."

"Now, I'm really going to go in and do some work. See ya." He turned away.

"Why don't you come for dinner when you can? Hannah and the kids would love to see you," Demarion yelled after him. "It'll take her mind off baby Rafael for a few minutes."

Michael called back over his shoulder, "I'll think about it."

As he went back the way he'd come, Michael's mind fell on Christina. He hadn't thought about her in far too long. He wondered how she was doing way across the Atlantic. Their relationship had ended when she'd taken a position at IBM in Hong Kong. Sadly, even though it had been a shock, it hadn't been a surprise. They'd grown apart, and he knew the reason why: not enough love on either side to keep them together. He was sure she'd forgotten about him while he wished her nothing but success and happiness.

Now that Cassandra had appeared and he'd soon see her, he contemplated if there was a chance with her, and if there was … he froze in his tracks at the thought and the question: Would he dare take it? Because if he did, his life would change in every way imaginable. He was just settling into his hometown and 100 percent invested—literally and figuratively—into making it the kind of place not just the residents were proud off but people the state over.

Could he afford to take his eyes off the prize, even if it meant his gaze would be filled with the wonderful Cassandra? As he entered the cool recesses of the theater, he didn't have an answer, but he was more than willing to find out.

***

On the way to her sister's place in Mattapan, Cassandra Googled Michael Kiley, Boston theater owner, and what she found made her catch her breath.

"What?" Talia glanced quickly over before centering her attention on her driving as she pulled the car around a black limousine SUV that had stopped in the middle of the block for no apparent reason.

"Michael once worked in Hollywood, as a writer—a successful one. I wonder why he didn't say something?"

"Maybe because it's in the past," Talia said breezily. "I bet he didn't tell you he was really rich too. He's the reason we also have the new restaurant and shopping pavilion and the upcoming medical center."

"Sounds like he's back not only to revitalize his hometown but to transform it."

"And I invited him to Dad's party tonight."

"What? You did not?" Cassandra turned to her sister, startled by the news. "Why?"

"Why not?" Talia shrugged, her gaze moving briefly from the road to her sister's prettily flushed face. "He wants to hear me DJ; Katelyn recommended me for the opening gala happening in a few days. So, I thought instead of giving him an EP of my work, he can hear me live tonight."

Cassandra didn't say anything, only felt the heat on her cheeks grow. She didn't understand why. Knowing she'd see Michael so soon had tripped her heartbeat and warmed her skin. She was not about to analyze it right now; she had too many other things on her plate and wasn't ready to add any more.

Talia wound her way up through her neighborhood and over to Ruthven Street where she pulled around back of a triple decker apartment house. As they exited the car, Cassandra saw the Mattapan trolley go by two streets over.

"I have to hurry up," Talia said, taking one of Cassandra's bags from off the back seat and handing it to her sister before grabbing the other out and slamming the door closed with a hip. She headed up the backstairs speaking over her shoulder, "I need to get to the hotel early, not just to do the music but to help Layla set up."

Following her sister up the narrow stairs to the third

floor, Cassandra asked, "How's she doing with her online event-planning business?"

"She's fine, though it's slow-going. She's taking a break to help organize your dad's party."

A question popped into Cassandra's mind and out her mouth before she could stop it, "Why can't Alex help her out?"

"Because"—Talia sat down the bag, quickly fished out her keys, and opened the door—"he's on maneuvers or drills or whatever it is."

Cassandra rolled her eyes. "When isn't he away? Or better yet: when is he home?"

"None of our business," Talia said and dropped the bag she was carrying. "Come on in."

Inside, Cassandra set her bag down on the living room floor of the two-bedroom apartment as her sister closed the door. Talia's place was neat, clean, and filled with more crates of vinyl records and CDs than with actual furniture. There was a small dining room and even smaller kitchen, perfect for cozy meals and early morning coffee.

"That couch is great; it's a sleep sofa," Talia said when Cassandra dropped onto it and sank comfortably back. "Down that hall are the bedrooms, one with a bed; the other has more crates and storage stuff."

"Thanks, though I might not have to use it; I'll probably decamp to the parents after the party. It's a great idea having it at the Boston Hotelier; they love that place. You'd better bring along lots of Frank Sinatra—you know how Dad feels about that guy."

"Old-blue-eyes forever." Talia rolled her eyes. "Okay, you want me to wait and give you a ride? I can give you an hour after I pack up everything and change."

Cassandra shook her head. "No, thanks; I'll Uber. For one, it's going to take me way longer than an hour to get ready. For another, I have to make a grand entrance, don't I?"

"If anyone can, you can." Talia grinned, and they

laughed.

The party was in full swing when Cassandra entered the ballroom by a back entrance and paused for a moment. She'd made good use of her time to glam up, though not as much as she would have for a Hollywood premiere; that is if she'd ever been invited to one. She took a few seconds to look around, for what or whom she wouldn't acknowledge even to herself, though she sure didn't see him. She smoothened down her perfectly fitted white V-necked dress with the tiny yellow butterflies stitched into the fabric. It made her feel totally proper and summery light. She took a deep breath, put a radiant smile on her face, and moved into the room proper.

Heads turned her way, with people pointing at her. Cassandra put a finger to her lips for those around her father not to alert him of her presence; even as a buzz of excitement went around the room as a few of the relatives snapped pictures of her with their phones. Most of them had been told she was out in Hollywood working so she wouldn't be making it to the party. Her father started to turn toward her even as her mother put a hand on his arm to stall him, but it was too late.

He turned, saw her, and froze in shock before bellowing, "Cassie," and scooping her up in a bear hug as the room erupted in applause. He sat her down before turning to his wife, Yvonne, perplexed. "Why didn't you tell me, Vonnie?"

"Happy retirement, Dad," Cassandra said through a sheen of happy tears as she kissed him on the cheek.

"I thought you were too busy to make it," he said, looking with bemusement from her to his wife.

"I wouldn't miss your retirement shindig for the world." She felt tears wanting to fall as she took in her father's happy grin. At sixty-seven, he still retained his head of dark hair though streaked with gray, his Italian ancestry clear in his chiseled features and dark blue eyes.

"It's wonderful you came all this way for me," he said before turning again to his wife, who hadn't said a word; she instead let him have this moment with his oldest natural daughter. "Can you believe our Cassie made it?"

"I can see her as clearly as you can, sweetie," Yvonne Chaletain said drily before taking her daughter in her embrace and whispering in her ear, "Thank you for happily surprising your dad."

Cassandra hugged her mother in return before pulling back and looking at her. A few years younger than her husband, she was startling attractive with sharp features and black eyes in her cocoa-colored skin. She was wearing a dress of a deep purple, her father's favorite color, that gave her dark skin a smooth, beautiful hue.

Picking up his glass of champagne, Cassandra's father raised it high. "A toast," he called, causing all the guests to raise their glasses in turn. "To family; *Alla famiglia* and retirement. *Alla famiglia.*" Everyone toasted and drank as Frank Sinatra sang "The Best Is Yet To Come."

***

Michael stood near the DJ stand staring at Cassandra. He couldn't help it; she illuminated the entire room. He'd known exactly when she'd entered through the back door—he'd been watching for her while trying not to. He'd hardly noticed the other guests arriving or even when her sister Talia had come in and started playing the music.

He'd been concerned about seeing her again, believing she wouldn't be the person he thought she was but someone he'd mostly made up. Yet here she was, better than any fantasy he'd ever conjured up; she was real, and she was lovely.

***

Cassandra's father introduced her to his many former

co-workers and friends whom he'd told all about "his daughter, the actress." A few asked if they could take pictures of the two of them, and the duo gladly obliged.

After a while, Yvonne called her other two daughters over for family pictures. Talia left her DJ duties safely with Katelyn, while it took a little longer for Layla and her two children—six-year-old Lexxie and eight-year-old Nicholas—to appear.

It had been a long time since Cassandra had seen her youngest sister. Though both she and Layla were similar in coloring, with creamy skin and hazel eyes, this was where the similarities ended. They were the opposite in every other way.

Once the family pictures were taken, the young women toasted their father with everyone looking on.

When the toast was over, Cassandra grabbed up her niece and nephew, two of her favorite people in the world, and planted kisses all over their faces until they squealed with giggles. After a few minutes, she turned her attention to her other sister. "How have you been, Layla?"

"Fine. I'm glad you could make it for Dad," she said, then turned away to go. "I have to check on the food in the kitchen."

Cassandra put a hand on her sister's arm before she could move. "You did a great job arranging all this by yourself."

"Talia helped when she could," Layla said.

"And the rest you did yourself because Alex is away … again."

"He's on a drill weekend."

"Of, course he is."

Layla frowned at her. "What's that supposed to mean?"

"Hey, it's Dad's night, so don't—"

"Don't make it about you and ruin it," Layla said before turning and walking away.

Cassandra stood there looking after her sister in consternation. After a few seconds, she let her eyes rove over the guests and caught sight of Michael, who stood talking to Talia. He turned in her direction, and their eyes collided.

Stepping away, he walked over to her. "Hello, it's nice to see you again," he said. "Other than you, Talia, and Katelyn, I don't know anyone else here."

"That was my younger sister, Layla, going in the opposite direction; sorry, I didn't get the chance to make introductions. You look presentable," she said, wincing inwardly at the word, one of the most serious understatements she'd ever uttered because he looked more than presentable; he looked beautiful.

He was dressed in a dark gray suit that could only have been tailor-made for him because of how lovingly it fit his footballer's frame. Underneath he wore a crisp white shirt; the top two buttons were open, revealing his strong neck and throat. His dark hair and beard were expertly trimmed, highlighting the clearness of his eyes, which were fastened on her.

"While you look wonderful," he said, taking in her soft white-and-yellow sleeveless dress.

"Let me introduce you to my parents. They'd love to meet an old friend of mine." She grabbed his hand and led him over to where her parents were seated. Cassandra introduced him to her father first, "Dad, this is Michael Kiley; we went to school together."

Mr. Chaletain gave Michael a brief once-over before putting out his hand.

"Congratulations, sir," Michael said as they shook hands, "on being newly retired."

"I've seen your picture in the newspapers. You were standing beside Mayor Thomlinson at that dedication of the Times building."

"The mayor likes taking lots of pictures. I hope you enjoy your days now that they're your own."

"Mom, you remember Michael from high school, don't you?"

"That was a while ago, Cassandra," said Mrs. Chaletain politely as she studied him curiously. "I've read about you too. I even saw you at that dedication ceremony."

"Did you have a good time when you were there, Mrs. Chaletain? We tried to make it a nice event."

She shrugged. "It was all right." She said nothing more, yet her watchful gaze moved wordlessly but meaningfully between Michael and Cassandra.

Standing next to Cassandra's mother was her sister, Zenobia, her mother's only sister, there was also Uncle Vance; their parents having passed away long before. They called her Auntie Z, and after introductions were made, her aunt said to Cassandras in a low voice, "Your friend seems nice."

"And it's nice to see you," Cassandra said. "Glad to see you haven't changed very much."

"Never, sweetie. When you get a chance, come by my table. Lynette's here, she would want to say hello; you two used to be so close. Your other cousins would love to see you too; it's been way too long."

"Of course I will, Auntie."

Before she moved off, Auntie Zenobia said mischievously, "Enjoy your time at home, though there's no doubt about it if you'll be spending it with that Mr. Kiley there."

After the two men chatted a few minutes longer on the state of Massachusetts' public golf courses, Cassandra and Michael started to walk away when they realized Talia had changed the music from a Latin Beat to the disco reigns of Diana Ross singing "Love Hangover."

"Want to dance?" Michael asked and held out a hand; Cassandra took it knowing he would be a great dancer, and onto the dance floor they went.

CHAPTER SEVEN

A few minutes later, Cassandra knew she'd been right: he was a terrific dancer; he was inventive and fun; his steps were smooth and coordinated and matched hers as they hand-danced, from close to back then close again. His cologne, set in motion by his body heat, was manly and inviting, pulling her in and making the blood rush to her head and other parts of her body she'd almost forgotten were alive.

They danced to more Diana, then Boyz II Men, then Whitney, Cassandra even managed a dance with her dad to one of his favorites "Staying Alive" by the Bee Gees. He acted his role as Tony Manero, the disco king, and they had fun.

After her dance with her dad, she danced once again with Michael, until they were breathless and needed a break. "How about something to drink?" Michael asked. "Or something to eat? The buffet seems to have everything the heart and the stomach would desire."

"Definitely, something to drink with ice," Cassandra said, and they moved over to the well-stocked bar. "Thanks, I haven't danced like that in a long time—it was fun. Once, I was in the background of a dance party show and it was so dark on the floor, I ended up stepping on my dance partner's feet, and we both fell down."

"You weren't hurt, were you?" Michael asked. "Lemonade? Or something stronger?"

"No, that's fine. I wasn't hurt physically except for my pride. I thought I had the moves of a Fly Girl." She put her arms up on the bar and one of her elbows struck hard, sending a ping up to her fingers. "Yikes." She rubbed the spot. "I hit my funny bone."

"Ow," Michael commiserated. "Not funny at all. Wait a minute." He reached inside his coat pocket, took out a crème linen business card and ink pen, then scribbled quickly on the blank side of the card before holding it out to her. "In case you want another theater tour."

Cassandra took the card and popped it into her purse. "Where's your phone?" she asked.

Michael took his phone out of a pocket, unlocked it, and handed it over.

Cassandra quickly typed in her phone number before handing it back. "It's only a fair exchange.

"Too true," Michael agreed, then, "Would you like to sit outside for some air?"

"Yes, I would love a fresh breeze." She pointed at her feet. "These heels look fabulous but were made by demon elves."

They exited the hotel onto the patio that was lit softly by moonlight and took seats at a table, which looked out over the harbor and the glowing Boston skyline.

"Do you enjoy your work out in Hollywood?" Michael asked.

Cassandra looked out over the water. "Yes, or at least I used to."

Michael nodded. "If there's any place in the world not to feel satisfied, to be unfulfilled, to be miserable, it's Hollywood."

"Oh, right," she said and took a sip of her lemonade. "You were out there as a writer."

"I should have told you, but it's in the past. I was middling as a writer and doesn't seem important anymore, except for the fact I've never met so many unsatisfied, troubled, reckless, unstable folks in my life than I did living in Tinseltown."

"It's not for the faint of heart, that's for sure."

"Though the place draws people who could probably be called clinically insane," he said, "it's amazing how many of those human failings have created some of the greatest performers in the world; who've given us some of the best performances of all time on film and television that millions of people—including me—love. It's the one thing we can be thankful for."

"True, I never thought of it that way," Cassandra said and looked at Michael in a new light.

Yes, he was a handsome man: Idris Elba, The Rock, and Colin Kapernick all rolled into one. Yet, he was also compassionate and intelligent with a great sense of humor. He was the kind of man who could sweep you off your feet, even if you didn't believe in Prince Charming and knew fairy god-mothers had been replaced by self-love and self-help.

"You think you'll ever go back?"

He shook his head without hesitation. "Never. My life is here." He gestured out at the Boston skyline. "There's the city proper: it's a major, world-renowned tourist attraction with Roxbury seen as only a neighborhood when it's much more than that, Cassie. It's a thriving community, a city within the city, a small town with folks who've lived there all their lives and so have their children and grandchildren, and they all deserve to live in a place that has affordable healthcare centers, where food insecurity isn't a problem; where climate change is addressed …" He suddenly broke off. "You know we can go down the list, Cassie, but it'll take all night."

"You have big dreams."

He stared at her. "I bet you do too."

She nodded. "Yes, I do."

At that moment, the doors leading out were pushed open and her father was there. "I was looking for you. The

Stewarts are here, Cassie," he said excitedly. "You remember them? They moved to New Hampshire three … no, four years ago. Come on, they want to say hello."

With a "you understand" glance at Michael, Cassandra got to her feet with him following suit.

"Time to shine," she said.

"I'll go see what your sister has on rotation. I'll see you later."

***

Michael followed them inside and watched for a moment as the Stewarts from the Granite State, two hail-and-hearty looking elderly people, greeted Cassandra enthusiastically. He didn't blame them one bit; he'd been just as happy to see her.

Something knocked against him from behind, and he turned. Cassandra's younger sister, Layla, had inadvertently bumped him with a utility cart.

"Sorry," she said, sounding distracted. "It has a bad wheel."

"Let me try and fix it."

Michael bent, raised the cart up on one side, and straightened out a disconnected piece of metal on the left back wheel.

"It should go steady now. Here, tell me where you need it to go."

"That table over in the corner." She pointed. "I'm packing up those gifts and putting them in the car."

With Michael's help, they placed the rest of the presents on the cart and took them out to her car, where they companionably stowed the gifts in the trunk.

"Thanks for your help," Layla said.

Michael thought she sounded exhausted. "It's a great, party."

"You think so?" She smiled briefly.

"Your parents are enjoying themselves."

She stared at him curiously. "Who are you?"

He put out a hand. "I'm Michael Kiley, and you're Cassandra's sister Layla. You two favor each other."

"And that's where the likeness ends."

Michael didn't reply to that; he said instead, "If you want to stay out here for a rest, I'll take the cart back inside."

"Thank you. I think I will. I'll follow in a few minutes."

"Take your time."

She stared at him. "You went to our high school. I think I remember you; you won the Harriet Tubman Scholastic Achievement Award two years in a row."

"Right," he said, surprised anyone would remember him winning those awards; he was prouder of those achievements than he was of any of the football trophies he'd won. "It was a long time ago." He smiled briefly. "Cassandra is lucky to have you, Talia, and your parents—a real family."

"There's my partner, Alex, too, and our children. He's just away right now," she said quickly. "His job and other obligations keep him busy."

Michael didn't comment, though he wondered where she and the children were on Alex's list of obligations. Suddenly, the voice of Beyoncé singing "Crazy In Love" was heard coming from the ballroom.

"Your sister'll have everybody out on the dance floor now."

Layla smiled for the first time; it was quick and brief. "No doubt, everybody will be up and moving."

With a nod, he went back into the hall. Layla remained outside for a while longer, taking a small respite from her life.

***

It was a couple of hours later that Cassandra was done being introduced by both her parents to people who'd obviously been told "all" about her or had seen her on a show or in a commercial—somehow. Feeling as if she'd lived up to the part of the glamorous-bubbly-yet-grounded daughter, and the need to be so "on" had lessened, she decided it was safe then to enjoy what was left of the party. She stopped at Aunt Zenobia's table as she promised she would. Every seat was occupied by her aunt, cousins—it was three of them—and their partners. They greeted her with hugs and shout outs that made her glad to see them too.

"Jerome," she said to her only male cousin. "Look at you with that beard and mustache." She rubbed his face. "You look like a teddy bear."

He laughed and pulled out a chair for her to sit. "It's good to see you." He introduced her to the young red-haired woman with green eyes who sat close to him. "This is Alexandria." Cassandra noticed a good-sized diamond pear-shaped engagement ring on her finger.

"Hi, Alexandria, nice to meet you."

"I love that dress," her cousin Lynette said. "It's been too long between visits."

"Way too long, and you look great, Lynn," Cassie said and looked at her cousin, who was a year younger than she was. Lynnette was a pretty woman with medium-brown skin and brown eyes, her hair a dark-reddish color braided to her waist. She was a tall, majestic woman with the confidence that intelligence and hard-working success had brought.

"It's really nice to see you too," Cassie said.

At one time, they had been as close as sisters. They used to go out to dance clubs together, the movies and hanging out with friends, enjoying each other's company. Yet, as time went by, they'd grown apart, and when she'd gone to California, that had pretty much been the end of their closeness, and the distance that was literally between became the only thing that remained.

Next to Lynette sat her sister, Jacqueline, and beside Jacqueline, Kenneth, her husband. Jacqueline was a more curvaceous version of her sister with the same coloring except her braids were shorter and with blond streaks.

"I saw you in a Tyler Perry movie," Jacqueline said. "At least I thought it was you."

"No, not me," Cassandra said. "And what about you two? How are the kids, Jackie? They all still look like Kenneth?"

"Every last one of them," said Jacqueline's quiet but affable husband with a laugh.

"They're huge, Cassandra," Jacqueline said, "it's all we can do to keep them fed."

"Nobody told you to have five boys," commented Lynette.

"You're going to have to come back for Jerome and Alexandria's wedding," said Auntie Zenobia, who smiled at the beaming couple.

"I knew that was an engagement ring—why didn't Mom tell me?" Cassandra asked, then to the couple, she said, "Congratulations, you two."

"It's recent," Jerome said, and took his new fiancée's hand. "By tomorrow, it'll be all around the family."

"Who was the guy you introduced Auntie Yvonne to?" Lynette suddenly asked Cassandra. "He's famous, isn't he? I know I've seen him before."

"No, he's not famous—" Cassandra began.

"He's definitely good-looking," Auntie Zenobia jumped in. "He's just an old friend of Cassandra's, and he's friends with the mayor too. His name's Michael Kelly."

"Kiley," Cassandra corrected.

Lynette snapped her fingers. "Ma, I knew I'd seen him before. He built the theater, gave money to the high school, and that's only two of his many giving projects."

"He's rich," Jackie said.

"You definitely have to introduce me now, Cassandra," Lynette said. "He seems single, has his own money—lots of it—and since you're going back to Los Angeles, there's no reason for him and me not to get to know each other, is there?"

"You two could talk about being business owners," Jackie jumped in enthusiastically. "Your construction company is a thriving business and woman-owned; one of the few in the city. You also give twenty percent back to student programs and your company is right down on Washington Street, not far from the theater. You and Mr. Kiley have a ton in common, sis." She turned to Cassandra. "You have to introduce them, cousin."

"So, when are you going to introduce us?" Lynette asked. "He's right over there with Talia."

"Before the night is out," Cassandra said and got to her feet. "Listen, I'd better go, I still have to stop over and say hello to Uncle Vance and Auntie Celia."

"You don't have to worry about them," Auntie Zenobia said with a wry twist of humor, "they're too busy at the buffet table; they won't be going anywhere until the food runs out."

Cassandra laughed. "It was nice seeing everybody, I'll see you all later."

"You won't forget, will you, Cassandra?" Lynette called from behind her.

"No, I won't," Cassandra assured her even as she wondered what she was going to do. Though, why she was wondering about it, she couldn't pinpoint. She would only be introducing Michael, her friend, to her cousin, who she'd always gotten along well with. There would be no harm in that, would it? Maybe the two would instantly like each other, hit it off so well they'd fall in love and …

They'd fall in love … and where would that leave her? In Los Angeles, of course, doing her acting thing, right? Right. So, why wasn't she happy to play match maker? Well, she just wasn't, and she wasn't going to examine why not at this moment either; she'd pass on any thoughts of introductions and falling in love; she wasn't here for that anyway. She would do only one thing: she'd find Michael, and only for one reason: he was the one she wanted to be with right now and she put that down to wanting to be around someone who really knew her.

She found Michael talking earnestly with her father's younger brother, Antonio, and rescued him.

"Excuse us, Uncle Antonio, Michael promised me another dance."

"Sure, sure," Antonio said. He was a robust, gregarious man, whose two loves were his family and his car dealerships. "Michael, I have six dealerships, and we sell from vans to cars all over New England."

"Have some more cake, Uncle Antonio; we'll see you later," Cassandra said, leading Michael away. "He can talk about his company for hours, days even."

Michael smiled as the lights lowered and the strains of "Make You Feel My Love" by Adele filled the room. Couples went out onto the dance floor and into each other's arms. Without a word, Michael took Cassandra's hand and led her out onto the floor and into his arms, where they danced slowly, his hands splayed strong on her back, her arms entwined tightly around his neck.

Feeling as if she couldn't look at him for fear of not what he'd see in his eyes, but what he might see growing in hers, she nestled her head beneath his chin, against his broad chest, and closed her eyes. She immediately felt something, and it almost brought tears to her eyes: she felt at peace for the first time in a long time.

CHAPTER EIGHT

It was after midnight and the party was starting to wind down when Cassandra walked over to where Talia and Katelyn were talking animatedly with Michael.

"Are you going over to the Carey's to continue the celebration?" Talia asked. "It's not that late." She turned, and with a smile at Katelyn, handed her a stack of LPs. "I think I'm going on home myself; I'm tired."

Cassandra glanced between her sister and Katelyn. "You need your space back. I'll call an Uber to the parents and sack out there for the night."

"No need," Michael said to Cassandra. "I'll be glad to drop you at their house if you want; I still remember where they live on Stuyvesant Street."

"Then that takes care of that." Talia clapped her hands happily. "I'll see you tomorrow, sis."

Feeling slightly bemused with no way out and not sure if she would have taken one even if it was offered, Cassandra told her parents she'd see them at home, and with a few goodbyes and hugs and kisses to a few family members and friends, she leaned against the nearest wall and took off her sky-high heels. Opening her bag, she pulled out a pair of flat shoes and put them on.

"Always come prepared, in case you gotta run for a bus," she told Michael.

He laughed. "I parked up the block. If you wait right—"

She shook her head. "No, I'll walk with you; it's nice out."

Outside there was still a slight breeze blowing as the moon shown full and brilliant. They walked slowly. At one point, Michael crossed behind her next to the street. They didn't talk for the first few minutes, only enjoyed being in the presence of the other on a warm, summer night.

"You miss it yet?" Michael asked, glancing at her.

"L.A.?" She shrugged. "It's so different from Boston, not like apples and oranges either—more like a beach umbrella versus a carburetor."

He smiled. "That's some comparison and surprisingly close to the mark."

"True."

"You know, I saw you a couple of times at parties."

"You did?" Cassandra stopped walking, surprised. "Why didn't you say anything, Michael?"

He shrugged. "I didn't want to bother you, and I was working a lot. I must of went to no more than three or four events in the time I was in L.A and I never stayed long at any of them—I left as soon as I got the chance."

Michael stopped beside a dark blue Audi E-Tron GT, opened the passenger door for her, and saw her settled in before going around to the driver's side. He got in and started the car with the press of a button, and glided it out onto the busy street.

"It would've been great to see you again, a friendly face. Why'd you leave—not the parties—Hollywood I mean?"

"They're better stories in the world than mine, Cassie."

"Make it a short story then; I'm intrigued."

She watched as he expertly maneuvered the car through the early morning traffic. She felt cocooned with him in its quiet, whispered luxury.

"It's short, nothing you probably haven't heard a thousand times before."

"Did you go right after high school like I did?"

"No, after Stanford. I thought I knew what I was doing, but I was naive, stupid, ambitious; prime prey for the Hollywood grist meal."

"Most of us were the same."

"Yeah, but I was drowning out there, and it took me more than ten years to realize if I didn't leave then and there, I'd never go and my soul would be lost forever. So, I grabbed what I could, went to the airport, and took the first flight out, and not once have I regretted it."

Cassandra stared out the window but didn't see the passing scenery, she was thinking about the tremendous effort of will, the positive sense of self it took to leave Tinseltown.

"I think about packing up and leaving L.A. all the time," she said.

"Why don't you?" Michael asked quietly.

She turned toward him and was surrounded by his presence in the closed confines of the car, with his clean smell and his low, smooth voice, the intimacy made her heart pick up a beat. She needed to get out of this car, or she'd reach out and grab him. In an effort to grab some semblance of control instead, she took a deep, calming breath.

"My family believes I'm out in Hollywood doing wonderful. They have no idea how incredibly hard it is trying to be everything for everyone."

"Instead of being yourself?"

She nodded, and to her horror, felt a tear trickle down her cheek that she quickly wiped away.

"It's all right," he soothed, and briefly squeezed her hand. "That place feeds off people's pain, obsessions and failings, Cassandra. And if you're like us—biracial—I mean, you're considered someone who gets over because of it, compared to someone of darker skin yet you're still not light enough to get the prestige parts. So, you have to deal with that while trying to know-who-to-know, to be liked well enough to get a job regardless of your talent, drive, and ambition just to get your foot in the door."

"Like high school," Cassandra said, and Michael laughed.

"You're a treasure, Cassie," he said, looking at her steadily. "You'll have the life you want, where you want; there's no doubt about it."

Cassandra, touched by his words, his faith in her, it shook her enough that she—for once in her life—didn't know quite what to say. She knew though that she didn't want to go home, she wanted to spend more time with this man.

"Do you—"

"You want to—" they spoke at the same time.

"You go ahead," Michael said.

"I was thinking it was still early, and it has been a long time since I've seen Roxbury at night," Cassandra said, "especially since it started on its revitalization journey. You mind a tour?"

"Not at all; let's go over to Nubian Square."

Michael maneuvered the car down a side-street and headed them into Roxbury proper and into the city's commercial center. Cassandra stared around at the changes that had been brought to the square.

"That's a huge Whole Foods." She pointed out the window at the store, which took up half a block.

"Fresh fruit, the freshest of fish as it should be. We still have Jones's on Dudley Street and the neighborhood stalwarts still shop there."

"New apartment houses," Cassandra noted.

"Many of those folks love the Whole Foods, but many more love having a choice; something they didn't have before."

Out the window, she saw that it wasn't just new apartment houses and grocery stores being added to the neighborhood, the older buildings and local businesses were being refurbished and rediscovered as well. There was a new police community center and a job training facility. Cassandra even noticed quality of life improvements had been added: secure lighting and planted medians in the streets filled with lush-looking plants and flowers.

"Would you like a drink—coffee or something else?" Michael asked.

"That sounds nice."

"I know a great place, popular, but won't be too crowded this time of night."

Michael drove a couple more blocks and pulled the car up into the valet area in front of a one-story building whose front walls were a vibrantly colored mural that looked as if it had been created by children. It was pictures of everything: grinning faces, rainbows, flowers, moms and dads, dogs, picnics—anything and everything all jumbled together.

A valet opened the car door for Michael, who got out and handed the man his keys. Michael then went around the car, opened the passenger door, and helped Cassandra out.

At the building's entrance, written on the sidewalk was the place's name: Carol's Coffee Bar and Lounge. One of the double glass front doors, shaded dark, was opened for them from the inside by a heavyset man, obviously security.

They entered a large spacious room backed by windows and booths; the rest was filled with small tables and chairs. The place smelled of apple martinis, fresh baked bread, and brewing black tea. The bar was set right in the center of the floor and served a combination of coffees, teas, and liquored drinks. A small jazz trio played quiet tunes in the corner.

Cassandra noted a couple of doors of the room swing back and forth as people came and went carrying plates of food. Michael was right, the place was very popular and was packed with talking, laughing people obviously enjoying themselves.

Michael led them to a table off to the side, near the back. On top of the table sat a lazy-Susan filled with bowls of nuts and dried fruit.

They didn't say anything for a minute, until Cassandra, trying not to feel awkward, said something awkward, "Did you know almonds aren't nuts but seeds?"

"Seriously?" Michael said, surprised and interested. "I had no idea."

"Most people don't."

A waitress appeared at the table to take their order. Both ordered cups of pomegranate tea with glasses of water.

"This is a cool place," Cassandra said, looking around.

"Ever since it opened, it's been a popular night spot, and not just for the bar; I've been told they have some of the best oysters in town."

Cassandra made a "yuck" face. "That's okay, I'll stick with the tea. I'm impressed with how this place has grown; Talia told me about it, but I had to see it to believe it for myself. Too bad I won't be here long enough to get the full feel of the neighborhood."

"You won't extend your stay?"

"I don't think I can."

He looked at her levelly. "I guess we'll just have to give you a reason, ha?"

Cassandra didn't say anything else. She put a couple of almond seeds on her plate and pushed them around. When not listening to the jazz combo, which was pretty good, they talked, catching up on each other's lives.

"When was the last time you talked to Langston?" Cassandra asked about their only mutual friend. The three had been like the three musketeers in school—at least for a while.

"I talked to him a few days ago. I want to put a couple of his paintings in the theater's museum. He has a new house in town."

"The last time we spoke," Cassandra said, "he was exhibiting his work in Europe, which was amazing to me." She sat for a moment, gazing across to the lights of Boston. "Amazing we made it through school, and afterwards to now." There was some wonder in her voice.

"You're the one who held us together," Michael said quietly.

Cassandra's gaze moved back to him. "Not really," she said and let her eyes roam over his handsome face and strong body.

Michael had always been dependable and kind, and the years that had passed only seemed to enhance those qualities in him.

He reached out a hand and pushed a strand of hair behind her right ear. "I always like your hair down."

"My wild look," she said, thinking how soft and sensual his touch was.

"I guess we'd better go," he said. "I don't want your parents to think I kidnapped you or something."

"They won't."

They left the restaurant, and once in the car, Cassandra suddenly felt nervous, unsure how the ride was going to end once they got to her parents' house. Michael turned down Stuyvesant Street and steered the car to a spot in front of the house. He got out and opened the car door for her.

"Thank you for the bringing me home, Michael."

"You're more than welcome, Cassie."

They stood in the space between the car and the door, a breath away from each other. He put a large hand underneath the sweep of her and brought her toward him so that their bodies brushed against each other. He pulled her closer still as his lips settled softly on hers, his mouth opening and causing hers to open as his tongue tasted her slowly and with pleasure—for the first time in years. This kiss wasn't a boyish fumbling of hesitant beginnings and awkward testing, but a man's knowledge of how to please a woman and make it last.

Cassandra felt a jolt of delicious warmth spring a whoosh of moistness between her legs at his probing, and moaned low in her throat. Michael Kiley had made her feel that way—wet, warm, adored … and just from the touch of his mouth. What more could he do to her?

Michael brought both arms around her, pulling her closer. His instantaneous hard erection pillowed in the heart of life between her legs and made having to separate from him that much more difficult to do. She allowed herself a few seconds to bask in the moment before removing herself from his embrace.

"Thank you," she said softly, not meaning the ride.

Michael pulled in a harsh breath. "No, thank you."

They stared at each other awe struck until Cassandra whispered, "I'd better go inside."

***

Michael stepped back, as if being too near her was so volatile he couldn't trust himself. He nodded, and before he knew what was happening, Cassandra had stepped up close to him again, stuck out her tongue, and licked his visible throat between the unopened buttons of his shirt. He groaned, the sound near pain, at the moist touch of her tongue. He knew for a fact he'd never wanted anyone as much as he wanted Cassandra. Oh, how he wanted to pick her up, toss her into the car, and race home with her to his bed. Before he could put thoughts to action, Cassandra turned, hurried up the walk, the porch steps, and inside the house without looking back.

Michael stood at the car, head bent, one arm was outstretched while the other hand firmly gripped the door's handle, the only thing holding him back. It was a full minute until he was able drive off, knowing this would be one of the longest and loneliest nights of his entire life.

***

Inside, Cassandra dropped her bag to the floor and dropped down next to it with her back against the closed door. She felt as if she'd been through a whirlwind with

Michael, a hot and sensual storm, and she wanted more. She couldn't believe how wonderful he'd tasted and felt, and mixed with it was the disbelief that she'd cried in front of him. She'd never cried in front of a man other than her father, and once, on-cue, in some television show she could barely remember.

Being honest with herself—which she mostly, always was—she was attracted to Michael; no, definitely more than that: what she wanted to do was jump his bones so badly it made her catch a breath thinking about it. Not only because he was handsome, smart, and determined, but because he knew literally and figuratively where she was coming from and had been.

In high school they'd both been in the "non-group" due to their bi-racial identity—not white enough for one group and not Black enough for the other—and desperate to find a place they belonged.

As part of that non-group, for her, bullying and girl fights came with the territory; it was as if they were requirements. But even then, she'd been a standout with her boldness and brassiness that had gotten her out of more than her fair share of trouble. She'd also countered that constant, soul-destroying harassment by performing in every high school play that would have her. And she'd been pretty good too, desperately good in her own opinion, because she'd been desperate to belong somewhere, anywhere.

Michael had been one of her theater mates, though not as an actor as he'd said, but as production manager, writer, stage crew, and many times—as she thought about it now with a modicum of amazement—a confidant, a confessor, even a healer ... those girl fights could be brutal.

Back then, she'd had a serious crush on Michael but hadn't done anything about it because they had been such good friends, but now after meeting him again, being in his presence and that kiss! She understood she had a very serious problem, she could seriously fall in love with this man all over again.

Cassandra's phone rang, breaking her thoughts and making her jump. She dug it out, looked at the small screen, and answered, "Hello, Josh."

"Hey, Cassie, when are you coming home?"

"It's usually polite to first ask: 'Having a good time, Cassie? How's your family?'"

"Okay then, are you all right? Having a good time?"

"Yes, and I'm not sure yet."

"What?" his voice went up as if he hadn't heard her correctly. "You're not sure yet? About coming home? Why not? I thought you were anxious about your shoot?"

"Not anymore."

"I gotcha," he said slowly. "I had a great week and thought we'd go away for a few days when you got back. How about Turks and Caicos? We'd go swim in the ocean and just relax."

"No, Josh; I don't want to go to Turks and Caicos. As a matter of fact, you should go, but with someone else."

"What? You're kidding?" There was a long silence on the other end until he asked, "Is there someone else?"

"No," she said quickly, feeling heat flush up to her hairline as Michael's face pulsed across her vision. "It's everything."

She had been satisfied with their relationship, or thought she'd been with their jet-setting to beautiful places, attending fabulous dinner parties together, and their mingling with a few of the top-tier Hollywood royalty. It all had been easy and fun, but now, she wasn't sure if she wanted that anymore. She needed time to understand what she did want. Was it Michael? Was it love she'd had for him all this time? Of course it was, even if it was something she definitely did not need in her life right now.

"Just go, Josh, and have a good time."

"I don't understand what' s going on here with you," he sputtered three thousand miles away. "One trip to Boston and all of a sudden you're different."

"No, not really, just finally being myself. Maybe we'll see each other when I get back."

She clicked off, and with a sigh of relief, gathered her bag and headed up the stairs to her bedroom.

CHAPTER NINE

After Michael had dropped Cassandra safely at her parents', he went home himself, taking the long route in an effort to calm down his body. He went to bed as soon as he arrived, but couldn't sleep; his mind was too filled with her, while his body ached for her.

Realizing laying there alone wasn't doing him any good, Michael got up and wandered restlessly through his brownstone. His home was situated in the expansive neighborhood of Beacon Hill. He'd inherited the apartment from his father along with a house on the North Shore in Manchester by the Sea, and a lot of money. He'd grown the money into so much more that he wouldn't be able to use it up in ten lifetimes, though he was giving it one hell'va shot by helping build clinics, commerce centers, climate-stable housing, and theaters in his beloved Roxbury. He was even considering selling the brownstone and buying a home in their old neighborhood on Dudley Street, where his mother had lived until she died.

He walked through the large library, through his office, then the dining room, and finally through the designer kitchen and out the patio doors into the quiet, enclosed garden. It was still warm out as he took a turn, then another, around the plants and flowers visible because of the streaming moonlight. Thinking about his mother made him wonder how she would have liked Cassandra; he felt she would have loved her—for her warmth, sense of humor, her generosity, the same as he did. The thought stopped him cold in his tracks at this sudden, shattering revelation.

Whoa, Michael, you're getting way ahead of yourself. He'd cared about Cassandra, of course, probably since high school. But that had been kid stuff, hadn't it? He'd wanted her badly— definitely—to the highest degree … there was no question about that, but had it been true love?

The answer was simple: yes. The realization that it was so simple made him sink down abruptly in the hammock stretched between two birch trees, and slowly let it sway him and his thoughts. So, what was he going to do about it? He would not scare her, that was for sure. He would take it one step at a time and see where it led, if any place. For one, he would show her how talented she really was; it would be a shock to her, but he hoped a wonderful one. Yet, that didn't truly answer the essential question, did it? Would he let his feelings carry him away, which wouldn't be like him, but there was no one else like Cassandra, was there? Or should he hold back and go slow and see what happens. Maybe it wasn't meant to be? *Just go with the flow like the kids used to say*, he told himself.

Cassandra would be going back to California soon enough, determined to be a successful actor. She deserved to follow her own star and not let anyone stand in her way, including him … right?

He fell asleep in the hammock without realizing it and without an answer to what was possibly the most important question of his life.

***

The next day Cassandra woke, thinking immediately of Michael. She lay in bed, her fingers at her lips as she remembered their kiss, then her kissing the warm skin at his throat. She couldn't believe she'd done such a thing.

Suddenly frustrated, she sat up and thumped the pillow. Did she really need this in her life? The answer was *no*, of course not, because it made her feel vulnerable and helpless, feelings she didn't appreciate for a second. It felt as if a big wave was coming her way, and she was helpless to stop it. Whatever this was becoming, she didn't need it now, so the best thing to do was stay away from it … from him.

She decided right then and there to spend the entire day with her parents. She got out of bed, showered, and after downing a piece of cinnamon toast and black coffee, she started early with her mother. She found her outside picking vegetables from her extensive garden that took up half of the backyard, which she'd fenced around and draped over with white sheets that ruffled in the breeze. After being directed to go back inside for garden gloves and a sunhat, Cassandra got to work picking food in whatever row her mother directed her to.

The last time she'd been home, her mom had been growing collard greens, tomatoes, and parsley; now, she seemed to have some of everything. There were rows of squash, green beans, okra, lettuce, carrots, kale, and other vegetables she couldn't name along with rows: strawberries and rhubarb, which her mother insisted was a fruit, while Cassandra wasn't so sure.

The two women worked side-by-side and companionably, with Mrs. Chaletain directing Cassandra on how to correctly clip stubs of okra without getting stuck with their tough, short barbs.

They were both picking tomatoes off their stalks when her mother asked, "So, you're doing okay in Los Angeles?"

"Yes, okay," Cassandra said with a touch of wariness. "Why?"

"There's no harm in asking, is it? I trust you to follow your own path, Cassie. It's just nice when all my children are in the same state, that's all."

"Sure it is, Mom."

Instead of the statement getting her back up like it

usually would, she decided not to take it too personally, which was a switch.

"I know it's old-fashioned"—her mother's gaze was on her task, pulling the ripe fruit expertly off the stalks, which were heavy with it—"but I can't help how I feel. Just seeing you all together—us together, as a whole family—was something I'd wanted for a long time."

Time, it occurred to Cassandra, that was what this was all about. Her mother was getting older, with Dad retiring and the grandbabies almost into double digits; all those adages about time applied here: it wasn't on their side; it moves at the speed of light and it waits for no man or woman. No wonder her mother was sounding so melancholy; she was worried about it "running out" and not getting to enjoy enough time with her family.

"It's great being here, in the old neighborhood, seeing everybody and hanging out with the relatives."

"But you aren't staying," her mother said and picked up a small spade she used to dig in the dirt around the plant.

"I can't; I have a life in Hollywood."

Her mother stopped digging, and for the first time, looked at her. "Do you, Cassie?"

"Yes, and I'm sorry … " She stopped, not sure what she was sorry for; living a life she'd chosen since she was a teenager? Yet did she have a truly satisfying life? Was it all she wanted? So far, coming home and meeting Michael again had stirred up feelings in her she hadn't known were there, confused, all-over-the-place feelings, but what was there to do about it?

"We're all fine, Mom; everything's going to be all right."

Her mother looked at her. "Is it?"

Cassie nodded, though she was not so sure herself; there were too many confused thoughts stirring in her head that had nothing to do with her family.

Later on, that day, Cassandra sat in the backyard with

her father, just the two of them, drinking lemonade and riffing on his retirement and all the things he'd always said he'd do when that day finally came versus what he would actually do: watch all the game shows he could stomach.

They talked and laughed making Cassandra realize how much she'd missed this, and especially him. It had been such a long time since she'd spent any quality time with her father, and the fact that he now had the time meant he—and she—were getting older, so moments like these were more precious.

"I'm glad you could make it home," her father said as he rocked in his chair, gazing out at his green lawn he took pride in still cutting himself. "It was a wonderful surprise, and the party wouldn't have been so grand without you there. Seeing you and having everyone there—it was truly special. I'll never forget it." His words sounded melancholy.

"You deserved it; we love you, Dad. Now, tell me what other plans you have now that you call the shots?" she asked, taking in his graying beard and his dark, thick hair streaked with gray—his pride and joy. She'd inherited his hazel eyes and was one of the reasons she considered them her best feature. "Other than becoming a game show aficionado. You can do whatever you want."

"I plan on relaxing, taking a few trips, those are my plans, I mean. Then there are your mother's plans."

"What are hers for you two?"

"She hasn't told me yet," he stated matter-of-factly, "but when she does, I'm in." He turned to his daughter, his gaze questioning. "What about you? I know I don't"—he searched for the right words—"meddle in your lives."

"You've never given us a hard time about the lives we lead."

"Your mother, she's always been the go-to one." He shrugged. "I don't know, maybe because you all were girls and I believed—still do—she's the best to give advice, more understanding of the nature of things."

"On some things, Dad, yes. But you're the one we came

to when our feelings were hurt or when we needed a hug."

"I know, but my grandest wish is that you and your sisters find happiness and the kind of love that will see you through everything and anything. The kind I have for your mom, what my parents still have to this day."

Cassandra looked away from him, having no choice but to tell him the truth. "I don't know if that kind of love exists anymore, Dad."

He stared at her. "Cassandra, when the right two people find each other, it exists." He sipped at his lemonade, then grimaced. "Do I wish this was a nice, cold beer."

"It gives you heartburn."

"Think of it, newly retired, and I should be able to laze around, staring at the television all day, drinking whatever I want. Yet can't drink a beer, because it doesn't agree with me."

They were silent for a few moments until he finally said something Cassandra wasn't expecting. "That Michael Kiley, he seemed nice."

She looked off. "He is nice. We were friends back in high school."

"He looks as if he wants to be more than friends with you now."

"Come on, Dad, you're running the risk of stepping in Mom's territory when commenting on your daughter's love life."

"Love, is it?" he said, then put up his hands in surrender as Cassandra frowned at him. "Okay, I'll stop. I know what I am: the fixer of leaky sinks, the driver to the grandkids' soccer matches, and the one your grandparents call if they run out of heating oil. Speaking of your grandparents, you should visit them while you'll here; they'll love to see you, and they're not getting any younger either. Your grandmother said the other day how nice it would be to have you home."

"No problem, I'll go over before I leave."

"Well, you might leave in the next couple of days or even

a day if you get a call from your agent about a big part and have to hurry back."

That is so not going to happen, Cassandra thought, wanting to laugh out loud while at the same time cry at how her father believed in her so much. It would never cross his mind she wasn't an in-demand actor.

"I will definitely go tomorrow, early."

"Good."

They sat companionably for a little while longer, enjoying the sun and the day and each other.

Later on, her mother sent her over to Layla's house to retrieve the children. When Cassandra pulled into the driveway, Layla's partner, Alex, was backing out into the street. He waved briefly, distractedly at her, and went on down the road. She parked, got out, and walked to the door where she knocked and waited a full three minutes before it was opened.

Layla stood there, a harried, surprised frown on her face. Under one arm she held a laundry basket full of tiaras, friend-of-the-bride sashes, and packages of pink-and-white balloons.

"Ma sent me to pick up the kids," Cassandra said, trying to quell any automatic defensiveness she felt at the frown.

"I could've dropped them off."

"It's no problem. Where was Alex off to?"

"A union meeting, I think."

"Are you going to let me in, Layla? Or should I wait for them in the car?"

"Oh, right," Layla said with a distracted air and stepped back. "I'm putting together a bachelorette party for tonight and still working on all the details."

"You need any help?" Cassandra stepped into the house.

The front door led into a small Spanish-styled foyer and down into a sunken living room used only for company. The house was a family suburban and meticulously clean. Cassandra had always been in awe of Layla's aptitude for juggling ten things at once and making it look effortless.

"No, I got it, thanks. I'll go hurry them up, Cass. I need to make sure they at least brushed their teeth." She set down the basket and headed for the stairs, calling over her shoulder, "There's coffee if you want."

Cassandra checked out the things in the basket and picked up a pretty white-and-gold-printed sash that read: *Bride-To-Be*. Layla should be wearing one of these sooner rather than later; her sister would make a beautiful bride.

Cassandra heard Layla trying to calm the excited voices of her niece and nephew as they got ready, and wandered into the kitchen where the lunch dishes sat neatly in their racks, the breakfast table de-cluttered and the oven spotlessly clean. She stopped at the entrance of her sister's work room; the only place in the house that was disorganized, with boxes, racks, cabinets, and bags of material her sister used in her event planning business.

"Cass," Layla said from behind her, "they'll be down in a minute."

"Your business seems to be doing well."

Layla passed by her and began stacking small boxes from the floor up onto her work counter. Cassandra bent to assist her.

"It's okay, I got it."

Cassandra straightened reluctantly, knowing perfectly well how much her sister hated any kind of help.

"When is Alex coming back?"

Layla froze, putting colored packages of streamers into a drawer. "Don't start, Cassie; I can't take it right this second."

She turned, and Cassandra saw that her sister's eyes, were large with tears. Layla was doing all she could—was digging down deep within herself—to keep them from shedding, from letting out emotions that were barely held in check. Cassandra, understanding, backed off, not wanting to make her sister's life harder than it was, even as it took everything in her to stop herself from grabbing Layla in a fierce hug and not letting up.

"I won't, but if you need anything, please tell me. The kids will want to stay with Mom and Dad tonight. Is it all right? I'll bring them back tomorrow after breakfast—I'll even make them my famous cinnamon toast."

Layla did something she didn't do often enough, she smiled.

"I heard about your toast, sprinkled with double helpings of sugar."

"Triple, then I tell them to go find Grandpa."

Layla laughed. "Thanks."

"Anytime, and I mean that."

They heard the children racing down the stairs and bounding down the hall. When they saw Cassandra, they double-teamed her with a volley of questions she refused to entertain until they got going.

"Not one word, you monsters, not until we get to your grandparents' house."

She herded them back down the hall with Layla trailing behind them. At the door, they grabbed up waiting backpacks (Trolls for Lexxie and Star Wars for Nicholas) and the three exited the house on a chorus of "*Bye Mom*s."

"Love you. And mind Gram and Paw-Paw," Layla said.

After Cassandra settled and belted the two children in the backseat, she got into the driver's side and started the car. Layla was still at the door. She waved once before turning and going back inside. Cassandra thought she'd never seen her sister looking so lonely and wished she could help. Cassandra knew she didn't want to end up that alone herself.

And would do everything in her power not to let that come to past.

LORELEI HENDERSON

CHAPTER TEN

That evening, Talia picked Cassandra up for dinner along with two of her old friends she hadn't seen in years but kept in touch with mostly through Twitter/X and Instagram. They were the first to arrive at one of her favorite restaurants in the Boston seaport district and ordered glasses of white wine while they waited for the others.

Next to show up was Abigail Lee Williams, or Abby as she was always called. She breezed into the restaurant, causing a few heads to turn her way, and not because she was overly tall or short or unusual in any way but because she had no filter when it came to her joys or agonies.

When Abby caught sight of Cassandra, she screamed across the restaurant. "Cassandra, you're skinnier than on TV."

Ignoring the comment, Cassandra stood when Abby reached the table and gave her friend a hug. When they were both seated, Abby greeted Talia, "Hi, Talia, aren't you glad your sister's back home?" Not waiting for an answer, she looked around for the waitress, saw her, and signaled her over. "I want at least one tall cocktail as a treat for getting here on time and not letting my dependents hold me back."

They gave the young woman their meal orders and as she departed, Cassandra looked at her old friend. She realized Abby, with her dark blonde hair, dark eyes, and tidy neat figure, hadn't changed much over the years; she was still energetic and as dedicated to her second husband and newly blended family as she'd been to her first young marriage.

"How's everyone?" Cassandra asked.

"The same," Abby said excitedly." Oh, wow, I forgot to text you: Megan got into BAA." She grinned at her old friend. "Theater major."

"Another actor," Talia said.

"We hope. Her idol's Issa Rae," Abby added quickly, "And, of course, you."

Cassie shrugged at the "and," surprised she didn't feel anything at all at not being included. Being who she was and had always wanted to be suddenly seemed impermanent, maybe even irrelevant; something she'd never thought she'd feel about her chosen profession.

Abby suddenly changed the subject, "You got the invitation to my party tomorrow night, didn't you, Cassie? Well, it wasn't an actual invite—it was a message to your email."

"I rarely read my email—you know that, Abby. I must have missed it."

"You can't miss this," her friend nearly wailed. "I told everybody you were going to be there."

"Why, Abby?" Cassandra tried not to sound as annoyed as she felt. "No one could care less if I showed or not."

"You're wrong. Cheryl's going to be there. Joel and Gary are coming."

"Tell her you'll be there, sis," Talia chimed in. "Michael will be there, won't he?"

"I don't know." Cassandra tried to make the words sound nonchalant, maybe even uncaring as Michael's face flashed in her mind. "I'll see how I feel tomorrow."

"Great, around seven-thirty," Abby said as if the matter

was settled and Cassandra would definitely be there with bells on. "It's going to be one of my best soirées."

Joel, the third member of their long-time-friendship, arrived at their table, keeping Cassandra from commenting on the fact Abby said this about every party.

"Hi, everyone," he said in an exaggerated voice of exhaustion as he sat down heavily in the unoccupied chair next to her.

"Hey, Joel," Cassandra warmly greeted the man, who reached over and kissed her cheek. "I thought you'd be here before us."

Joel, heavyset with gray hair and affable features in his caramel-colored skin, rolled his dark eyes. "I had to take the T, such a nightmare during the evening rush."

The waitress appeared with their drinks and took Joel's order.

Abby raised her orange and red cocktail to him in acknowledgment. "What a thing to say with you being a chief streetcar inspector."

Minutes later, the waitress and a helper appeared with plates full of lobster and fresh corn. Donning bibs and with nutcrackers in hand, they expertly went to work on their meal. They'd grown up eating the crustaceous; they were as used to them as mother's milk, so they enjoyed the experience of cracking, pounding, and digging for the sweet meat.

"I'd forgotten how challenging these things are," Cassandra said, dodging a squirt of lobster juice as she cracked a claw.

"How's Tinseltown, really?" Joel asked conspiratorially as he expertly used a pick to dig the last of the meat from a pincer. "I love keeping up with my only actor friend."

"It's the same, Joel."

He resoundingly dropped his fork and pick onto the table. "How can you say that so coolly?" he asked incredulously. "My life is so settled, it's sunk: go to work, come home, Gary and I have dinner, clean up, read or watch a show, then bed, only to do the exact same thing the next day and the next."

"What's wrong with that?"

"It's not movie premieres, award shows, or studio parties, that's what's wrong, Cassandra. My life is a million—a billion miles—from the kind of life you lead."

"Yeah, but its love," she said sincerely, meaning every word. "That's the kind of life you have, Joel.

They all looked at her, surprised, maybe even shocked by her words. She was shocked herself as she realized it was true. Wat her friends had in common was that they went home to love, and even though they complained good-naturedly, they wouldn't change very much at all. Her friends were Bostonians to their very hearts; New Englanders with their distinctive Boston accents, though their families hailed from Dominican Republic and Cape Verde respectively. They knew where they belonged and wouldn't leave this town even if given the chance.

After dinner, with hugs and kisses goodbye and promises to keep in touch, Talia asked, "You wanna go to the zoo?"

"What?" Cassandra stared at her sister. "Now? It's nighttime."

"The best time, and it's to raise money for the Frances Matthews Foundation and the new clinic. And it'll be the Boston Zoo Lights. You know how you wanted to see those."

"Yes, I know. So, let's go."

On the way to the Franklin Zoo, one of the country's oldest urban zoos, Cassandra asked, "What's the Frances Matthews Foundation?"

"Michael started it to raise money for the new clinic to be built in Roxbury."

Cassandra thought how wonderful that was and how terrific Michael was for doing something like that. It had been a long time since she'd met someone like him, a genuinely good person. They'd been friends for such a long time and now were friends again. Yet, she found herself wanting more when she shouldn't, and she silently chastised herself for the wanting. Here she was living miles away, supposedly focused on nothing but her career, yet wanted this man like she hadn't wanted anyone else. She was actually falling in love with Michael, and there was no doubt in her heart about it. What a lesson in bad timing this visit was turning out to be. *That time thing again*, she thought scornfully.

The entrance into the Franklin Zoo was decked out, as if it were for a New Year's Eve festival and grand carnival rolled into one. Talia pulled the car around to an area where a reserved flag swung from a pole. She parked next to a white Mercedes SUV, one of the few unoccupied spaces left in the lot.

"Should you be parking over here?" Cassandra asked.

"Absolutely," Talia said, hopping excitedly out of the car as her sister followed behind.

They moved along with the crowd up a path lit on both sides by arcs of lighted trees that sparkled in rainbow colors. Cassandra was already impressed with what she saw and they hadn't even gotten to the main entrance.

They heard Talia's name called and turned as their parents, with Lexxie and Nicholas in tow, hurried toward them. Their mother put Lexxie's hand into Cassandra's as their father gave over Nicholas to Talia.

"You're younger," their mother said, "and can keep up with these young'uns." She looked between her daughters. "You both look pretty this evening."

"Thanks, Mom," they said in unison.

As a family, they walked into the neon splendor of the world of a thousand lanterns in all shapes and themes. *The "wow" factor was well deserved*, Cassandra thought as she gazed in amazement at the swirl of lights depicting the EAC or Eastern Australian Current. The light currents swam speedily around and around with hundreds of fish, turtles, and jellyfish pulsing with color within as they flowed by.

Lexxie and Nicholas stared open-mouthed, making them all laugh.

Awed by the spectacle, they were eager to move on to the next lantern show and found themselves in 65 million BC, the land of dinosaurs. There were more than six of them, four of them were at least nine feet tall, and they moved and roared with delightful intensity. Cassandra compared them to anything Walt Disney had produced and found these just wonderful.

The lantern show was a big hit from what she could tell from the crowds that moved from one amazing depiction to the other. If the number of people moving back and forth were any clue, the fundraiser was already a huge success.

They heard Madonna's "Vogue" playing and walked toward it. Up ahead was a stage set up with a couple of tables. On one table sat gift boxes and bags, while on the other food and water. A standing mic was at center stage.

People were dancing to the music as attendants wearing Matthews Foundation shirts passed out plates of salad, sandwiches, and fruit while other ones handed out the gift bags and boxes. There was a banner over the stage that read: *Thank you for contributing*, and *Have a great time!*

"Eighties music," Talia said. "Not bad, though they need to cue up a mix of hip hop; some Tupac would get this party started."

Cassandra didn't respond. Instead, she watched as a man stepped up to the center mic and tapped it, causing enough feedback that everyone looked his way as the music stopped. The man was of average height and weight and had reddened with embarrassment.

"My name's Robert Brandt," he began. "The CFO for the Matthews Foundation, and I want to thank you, more than you know, for contributing to the medical center and for coming here tonight. We're overwhelmed by your response and commitment to making sure there is healthcare for all in Roxbury."

There was a warm applause and shouts of

encouragement as Mr. Brandt went on, "Michael Kiley is around back somewhere, and I'm going to get him up here to say a few words."

The applause grew louder as Cassandra took a few steps near the front. A few moments later, Michael walked up onto the stage and approached Mr. Brandt. Cassandra drew in her breath. Boy, did Michael look great dressed in a fitted, white polo shirt, blue chino pants, and dark blue suede sneakers.

He stepped up to the mic. "I'll make this quick, I promise. Thank you all for your time, your contributions; it means so much to this community we all love."

His gaze roamed over the crowd and halted on Cassandra, a warm heartbeat of seconds that touched her from head to toe.

"I hope you enjoy yourselves," he finished and waved as he left the stage to a spattering of applause.

More than a few people tried to spark up a chat with him, shake his hand, but he politely declined each instance and walked directly to where she waited.

"Cassandra, I'm surprised to see you—glad to see you."

"I'm glad to see you too, Michael. This whole thing, it's great."

"Hi, Michael," Talia said as the children echoed her greeting. "These kiddoes are getting restless, so we're going off to see what's around the next corner."

"I'm not going to tell you what's up ahead," Michael said, "other than it's terrific."

Talia hustled the children away, who were excited by the prospect of more awesome sights.

"Do you think the foundation will do really well tonight?" Cassandra asked.

"Definitely, we've already surpassed our goal. Would you like to see more of the show?"

Cassandra smiled. "I would be delighted, Mr. Kiley," and put her arm through his.

The next section they entered was a carnival of lights

shaped into a roller coaster, a carousel, even a Ferris wheel; they were delighted by the ingenuity of each light show they passed through. At one point they stopped, mesmerized by the one in front of them. Lanterns in the shape of round, blazing stars against the dark sky were strung strategically overhead, with swirls of white light pulsating through over a black, paper-machete city; a lighted sign stated it was a depiction of Vincent Van Gogh's *The Starry Night*.

"It's amazing," Cassandra said.

"Yes," Michael agreed, looking from it to her.

Cassandra grasped his hand turned to him. "I'm so proud," Cassandra began, "of what you've done and will—"

He put a finger to her lips. "My being with you, at this moment, is all that matters."

She nodded, and still holding hands, they stared at each other under *The Starry Night*.

CHAPTER ELEVEN

It was early morning when Cassandra made her way downstairs to make coffee for herself, knowing her parents would sleep in, at least for twenty more minutes now that they had no set schedule. She reveled in the house's quietness as the coffee percolated, and when it was done, she took a cup with her out into the backyard and sat at the picnic table. On one side of the yard was the refurbished playhouse and a swing set, a few yards away, the kiddy pool.

She stared across the side yard at the row of New England styled homes with their many rooms, multi-levels and wide, wrap-around porches. She'd missed this about Boston; the uniqueness of New England itself. Here there was room to breathe, where L.A. was so tight—sunny of course, but still tight—yet it was the place she'd chosen to call home.

A couple of hours later, after an uber ride to North Station, Cassandra walked down Lovejoy wharf to catch the commuter ferry over to South Boston. She'd promised her father she'd visit with her grandparents, and today was the day.

She could easily have taken the train or even a cab to get to her grandparents but had always—since a child—loved traveling by ferry, the epitome of the scenic route. To top it off, it was a perfect day to be out on the water. She'd made the reservations for the ferry online the day before so didn't need to stop at a booth or a stand to buy a ticket.

She stood on the jetty, clad in jeans, designer sneakers and a long-sleeved, yellow summer blouse, her thick sun-kissed hair loose as she waited alongside a group of tourists for the ferry to arrive. While waiting, she took in how Lovejoy and the surrounding area had changed.

For as far as her eye could see, new designer luxury apartment blocks and high-rise office buildings filled the skyline, accompanied by new boutiques and restaurants that appeared to be crowded with tourists and residents. It was a revitalization boom she hadn't expected, and it had greatly changed the area, she hoped, for the better.

Cassandra heard a small commotion from the tourist and looked out to sea; the ferry was gliding toward them, taking its time. It was another ten minutes before the boat, the *Donahue Dorsey* written on its side, pulled into the dock and its passengers disembarked. She was the last to board and took a seat inside the ferry's interior.

Once the attendant had come around and scanned the tickets from the passengers' phones, Cassandra went topside. It was a short trip to the South Boston seaport, and just as she used to do as a kid traveling over with her dad and Layla, she stood at the rail and watched the North Shore recede as the sun sparkled off the water and a breeze fluffed the waves.

As the boat plowed through the water, churning up foam against its hull, Cassandra watched them approach the North Washington Street Bridge and sail underneath, turning the breeze to cold as it bathed her body.

Other ferries and leisure crafts carting passengers plied the water around them, enjoying as she was, one of the best things about the city: the ability to get onto the water in a matter of minutes if you felt the need.

Not long after the bridge, a ski team of more than forty

people, stacked on top of each other in a pyramid shape, passed by the ferry, causing the passengers on deck to excitedly grab their phones and take quick snaps. *People love a show of just about any kind*, Cassandra thought before snapping a couple of pictures herself to show Lexxie and Nicholas.

A few minutes later, the ferry pulled into Fan Wharf in the Seaport District, and they exited the boat. Out on the street, Cassandra hailed a cab, but instead of having the driver take her directly to her grandparents' house, she told him to drive around the Waterfront Seaport.

"I want to drive around first, then head over to 642 Dorchester Street."

The driver glanced at her in the mirror with a bored look. "It's your dollars," he said in a voice just as bored.

He moved out in traffic and drove slowly around the waterfront. Cassandra was effectively amazed at what she saw; the changes were almost as impressive as what was taking place in Roxbury. There were new hotels, luxury apartment complexes, high-line restaurants, a park that looked lush and inviting, and even a promenade along the harbor.

"Okay," she addressed the driver. "We can head over to Dorchester Street now."

It was only a few miles from the Seaport to the house; she could have walked there if she needed to. The cab pulled up in front and Cassandra handed over forty dollars.

"Thanks for the tour and the ride."

She opened the door and got out. As the cab pulled away, she looked at the newly painted light blue house with its neatly cut lawn and pots of different colored dahlia's sitting on the porch steps; healthy looking plants and flowers also hung in baskets from the porch beams. Cassandra recognized this as her grandmother's doing and was glad to see it; it meant her gram was still able to tend her beloved plants, one of her all-time-favorite things to do.

Instead of going up to the front door, Cassandra went

around the side of the house and up the stairs to the back door. She knocked and waited patiently, knowing it took a few minutes for them to answer the door—they were in their late eighties and took their time. She heard motion on the other side before the curtain covering the door's wide window was pulled aside and her grandfather, Salvatore Chaletain, peered out at her. For a few seconds he just stared, then recognition suffused his face and, fumbling with the door's lock, he finally got it open.

"Cassie, you're a grand sight for these old eyes. Come on in here."

She stepped into the kitchen and was immediately struck first by one of the smells that defined her childhood: Gram's perfume, Anais Anais. Along with that smell were two others that swept her with nostalgia for home and family: the sweet smell of confectioner's sugar and hot coffee. She glanced at the stove and saw there was a fresh pot brewing; she knew it would be freshened again and again as the day went on.

"Hi, Grand," Cassis said as she hugged him gently, feeling his thinness of age as he returned her embrace. "How are you?"

"Come on, let me look at you," he said and stepped back. He grinned at her through his white beard. "You look like a ray of sunshine."

"You look pretty good yourself," she said, taking in his thinning white hair and beard and the deep crinkles that surrounded his fading blue eyes. "I'm glad I didn't catch you two sleeping in."

The old man's smile widened. "Ah, you know if we're not up at five, it's because we can't get up. Mary," he called excitedly, "we have a visitor."

"Who is it, Sal?" called a voice from the direction of the living room Cassandra knew well.

"Come and see."

"Salvatore, I'm busy—"

"Come on, Mary. It'll only take a minute."

They heard shuffling feet and a few seconds later, she was there in the doorway between the living and dining room, her grandmother, holding in one hand an extended feather duster taller than she was.

Mary Chaletain was gnome-like with short, white-blonde hair, and when her green-eyed gaze settled on Cassandra, she dropped the duster, the hand going to her heart in surprise before those green eyes (still bright) shimmered with tears as a welcoming smile softened her face.

She opened her arms wide, and Cassie went into them, her cheek resting atop the woman's head as she closed her eyes and breathed in her grandmother: Anais Anais, Abyssinian oil, and tea tree along with her own, unique "Gram" smell.

"Hi, Gram, I've missed you."

"I know, honey, because I missed you too."

Cassandra pulled back and let her gaze rove over her granddaughter.

"So, I watched that movie *C'mon C'mon*, and I saw you next to the girl in glasses."

Cassandra laughed out loud, suddenly thinking of Michael. Now there were two people in her life—and probably the only two people on the planet—who recognized her in the background.

"Thanks, Gram. Look at you, still chasing those pesky dust bunnies, ha?"

"Oh, you Cassie." The little woman reached up and kissed her cheek before grabbing her hand. "Sit, sit; you can stay a while."

Cassandra pulled out a kitchen chair from their round Formica table covered with its flowered cheese cloth, and once her granddaughter was seated, she pulled out one for herself and sat down.

"Sal, get the pasticiotti, made fresh yesterday."

Sal went over to the glass-fronted cupboard, took out three cups and saucers, handing them to his wife, before retrieving the cellophane-wrapped cakes off the counter and placing them on the table before seating himself.

"You want coffee?" Mary asked, getting up and retrieving the pot.

"What a question," Cassandra said, watching as Mary poured them all cups of her strong brew. "Why didn't you come to Dad's retirement party?"

"Your grandfather doesn't drive anymore, and we didn't want to have to depend on a ride. Anyway, we had dinner over there a couple of weeks ago, and that was enough."

Mary unwrapped the pasticiotti—delicate, small cakes filled with a fruity cream and dusted on top with white, confectioners' sugar.

"Pusties," Cassandra said, relishing the term they'd loved to call the small cakes as children.

"You always loved them," her grandmother said, smiling at her granddaughter's delight at the treat.

Cassandra picked up the delicate dessert and took a bite; it melted in her mouth, the cake moist and the creamy blueberry filing, sweet. "Gram, these are your best yet."

"Definite praise since you haven't eaten my cooking for a long time, granddaughter."

"And I've missed it. The blueberry cream tastes so fresh."

"Your mother brought me a basket full the other day."

"So, how have you two really been doing?" Cassandra's eyes jumped from one to the other. "The house looks kept up, at least the outside does. I'm going to snoop around once I'm done with my pustie."

"We're doing fine." Her grandmother waved the question aside. "Your dad is here every other week. Your aunt Grace and ancle Antonio come by when they can get down here—he makes sure there's plenty of winter heating oil. Though our fingers are crooked with arthritis, we're still holding fast to as much independence as we can."

"Your cousin Mara's near Carson Beach, in walking distance," Sal said. "She comes by when she can too. You know she had another daughter a couple of months ago?"

Cassandra nodded. "Mom told me; her fourth daughter, talk about busy."

"Her husband's what you kids today call 'hands on.'" Her grandfather rolled his eyes. "She's good, though it doesn't stop her complaining constantly about her life." He poured himself more coffee.

"How's life in Hollywood?" Mary asked eagerly. "You must be having a lot of fun, working hard in those movies of yours."

Cassandra shrugged. "It's all right."

Her grandmother looked at her keenly and stated, "You miss home."

"I miss you and Grand and everyone else." Cassandra picked up her grandmother's hand and kissed it before sandwiching it warmly between hers. "I love you both."

"We miss you too. You're our first grandchild, and we loved you on sight."

"It took us a little while longer with your mom," Sal added with a raised white eyebrow.

"Like a day or two," Mary said shortly. "Your mom's feisty and wouldn't give up on us. She pushed her way into our Southie hearts."

"We were never prejudice, you know," her grandfather stated pointedly as he always did when referring to first meeting his son's choice of bride.

"I know; just stubborn," Cassandra said. "And anyway, Mom's a pistol, she could take care of herself. Can I take a couple of the pusties home with me?"

"Definitely, they're too rich for your grand over there anyway."

"No, they're not," Sal countered. "But our Cassandra can have them all."

"Come on," her grandmother said. "I have something else for you too."

She got carefully to her feet and moved out of the kitchen, with Cassandra following behind. They passed through the ornate dining room with its huge, oak break front that had been in the same place since before Cassandra was born. Mary led her into the living room that was stuffed with furniture and floor rugs because her grandparents hated to throw anything out.

Cassandra walked around the entire room looking at the framed pictures that filled all the available space: generations of family and friends, almost too many to count. On the coffee table, among the crystal ash trays and cigarette boxes no one had used in years, sat an ornamental jeweled box. Mary opened the lid and took out what looked like a flat, silver box. She opened it, and Cassandra realized it was a two-sided picture frame.

"I found this last week when I was cleaning out an old wardrobe in the spare room." She held the frame out to Cassandra, who gently took it. "It's a picture of your great-great-grandparents—my grandmother, Saorise, and grandfather, James."

Cassandra gently opened the frame to a black-and-white photograph of what she thought would be separate pictures but was instead one of two people who weren't frowning or stoic-looking, liked she was used to seeing in photographs from the turn of the century. These two were smiling at each other, laughing, their bodies close together, their faces nearly touching, their fingers entwined as they looked into each other's eyes, clearly in love.

"I know how much you feel for family, and with you so many miles away from us, you can have this with you there. They took that right before they sailed to America, and at the time, they had nothing—James was an orphan, and Saorise's family was so poor, her parents couldn't afford to feed them all. They had nothing but love only proving: love is possible in all kinds of situations, a lasting love too."

"Oh, Gram; I can't take this, it's too valuable, too important to you."

"It's family, honey, and yes you can. It'll give you comfort until you come back."

"I'm not—"

"Now, give me hug," her tiny grandmother interrupted and threw her arms around her granddaughter's waist.

Cassandra laid her cheek gently against the top of Mary's head as Sal walked into the room, a covered Tupperware bowl in one hand.

"Your pusties," he said, and they all laughed.

They said their goodbyes before Cassandra made her way back to North Shore.

On the ferry ride to her parents', Cassandra took out the frame and looked at Saorise and James. She ran a finger over their faces where love shone out. Could this be real? That kind of love? Of course, it was, she saw it between her grandparents and her own parents but did that mean it was for everyone? Was it for her? She had never believed it was, at least not some bold, intense, all-consuming love, but maybe she was wrong and she considered this only because of Michael. She was definitely in love with him. She'd tried to stay away from him, had reasoned with herself how she had a life in California, yet here she was, in love with her friend. So what was she going to do about it?

CHAPTER TWELVE

That night, Cassandra pulled her dad's car as close as she could to the front of Abby's large, brightly lit house on Irving Street, in Cambridge, Massachusetts. The street was clogged with cars, though Cassandra saw valet services had been reserved for the function; a good move on her friend's part, she thought. Cassandra got out of her car and gladly handed over the keys to the smiling young man.

She stood on the walkway for a few moments smoothing down the peach-colored halter dress she'd worn to counter this evening's sultry weather; the dress hugged her curves down past her knees. She'd left her hair free down her back, its coloring a warm fire against her skin. When she felt prepared enough for the show to come, she mounted the front stairs and rang the doorbell.

The door was opened by Horton Williams, renowned professor of Computer Science at Harvard University and Abby's husband. Her friend had rebounded from a failed and miserable first marriage, had found and chosen Horton, whom Cassandra had thought was the best thing Abby had ever done.

"Horty." Cassandra threw her arms around the tall man, jostling the black-framed glasses on his nose. "You're the only person I truly wanted to see; now that I have, I can go back home."

"Abby'll have a fit if you escaped her and this crowd." He gently grasped her arm. "Come on in."

"It's great to see you; you never change."

"It's my hairline that does the changing."

Cassandra stepped into their beautiful entryway with its white-and-blue-checkered tiles. Tall vases of fresh flowers lined both sides of the hall, which led off in three directions. African hip-hop music—Cassandra recognized Burna Boy—flowed out all three rooms.

"I'm glad you could make it home," Horty said, "Your father must have been over the moon to see you."

"Yeah, he was pretty gobsmacked." She lowered her voice. "Did most of them show up?"

"You doubt they would?" Horty's question had a clinical ring to it. "There's plenty of food, endless drink, and the chance to see and be seen."

"That's what I figured." Cassandra sighed. "I'm gonna try and sneak through and get out fast."

"Your luck might hold out until Abby sees you."

"Okay, here goes."

She chose to go through the archway in the middle of the hallway, into one of the large lounges filled with party-goers. Inside the room, Cassandra saw that Abby had gone on a decorating spree since her last visit a few years before. There were now boldly colored sofa groupings and long blond-wood tables filling the space. Through glass doors, where walls had once been, Cassandra saw an in-ground pool; people stood around it bathed in its lighting; for a second, it reminded her of any party thrown at a luxury estate in the Hollywood Hills.

Abby and Horty had made a lot of changes since she'd been there last, and for some reason, this brought on a brief touch of sadness. It seemed everyone else was moving forward with their lives, building their futures, creating strong and lasting connections with their community and their families, while she was still chasing dreams she'd had as a teenager.

"I knew that was you …"

She turned as a familiar voice behind her brought her out of her revery.

"… the moment I saw that hair."

"Hey, Cheryl," she said, resisting the attempt to reach up and smooth down any errant waves and curls.

In high school (long before she'd learned to embrace her hair and it's unique attributes), it had been one of her features that had caused her trouble. Her hair had been too many things back then: long one day, curly the next, red on Tuesday, blondish-red on Wednesday, or all of those things at once; it had made her stand out too much.

To Cheryl's benefit, she hadn't been part of the group who'd given her a hard time over anything that seemed "too different." Cheryl had even tried to intercede against the bullying once or twice, to befriend her when it wasn't "popular" to do so. Cassandra regretted never letting her know how much it had meant to her.

"It is great to see you," she said with a meaningful warmth.

"You too, and not just on the small screen," said Cheryl, who was petite and pretty with her dark brown hair and large brown eyes.

"Our wanna-be-a-star has arrived," said a familiar voice they both immediately recognized.

As the woman stopped in front of them, Cassandra realized that her one wish—that this person wouldn't be at this party, because she was either out of the country or taking a trip on Space X—had not come true. Instead, here she was, Waverly Santos.

They had been so-called rivals back then, though Cassandra still felt that had been all wrong; it had been a stupid, teenage misunderstanding. And all because of one person, one guy. His name had been Oliver "Ollie" Armstrong. He'd been one of the coolest people in school because he'd been good with everyone. He'd had a mildly amused, self-confident air that had allowed him to be a hit with just about every group, gang, or clique.

He'd been basketball-player tall—though he'd played football—skin the color of cherrywood and sea green eyes. Girls, some of the boys too, had been crazy about Ollie. He'd had his choice of partners and had chosen Waverly— one of, if not the most, popular girl in their graduating class. They had been Roxbury High's version of Jake and Caroline from *Sixteen Candles* fame; they were the king and queen of school, and everyone had known it, including Cassandra. When Ollie needed an extra credit to graduate, he'd joined the theater club; he and Cassandra had gotten along like a house on fire, but only as friends. Yet, no one believed this was so except for Michael, who'd been one of the production workers. Everyone in the theater group had gotten along because everyone was accepted for who they were, including Ollie.

But Waverly had seen Cassandra and Ollie together a couple of times and assumed—wrongly—Cassandra was after him. For his part, Ollie hadn't tried to disabuse Waverly of this idea; he'd maybe even egged it on. Waverly had confronted her, Cassandra remembered, when leaving the lunch hall. Waverly and her crew of four friends had appeared in the doorway, causing everyone to halt their progress to class. She'd glared at Cassandra.

"You need to keep away from my dude," she'd said, then commenced to grab Cassandra by the hair.

They'd tussled a few minutes until they were pulled apart by a couple of teachers. Cassandra remembered losing only a few strands that time and thinking how lucky she was not to end up with bald patches. They'd both received a day's suspension. Cassandra had, of course, never forgotten it, and it appeared Waverly hadn't regulated it to the past either.

"I heard you might show," the woman said.

Waverly was still beautiful, Cassandra saw; she'd of course been a beautiful girl with her ash-blonde hair, gray eyes, and cheerleader figure. It was her bad attitude and sense of entitlement that made her a mess.

Waverly stepped in front of Cheryl, who stepped back.

"We must be the luckiest folks in the world," she said sarcastically, "to be gifted with your presence."

Cassandra instantly decided to play this as if she was really in a Tyler Perry television drama. "I'm thrilled to pieces that you noticed me. Listen, Waverly, I may not be in Viola Davis's league, but I am an artist. Yes, a background artist, but I work hard at giving it my best."

The woman's eyes narrowed dangerously on Cassandra, who wondered for an instance if this meeting would deteriorate to more hair-grabbing.

"Who could help it in that dress you're—" Waverly began but was cut off in mid-sentence by a male voice.

***

"You don't want to relive the bad old days, do you, Waverly?" Michael stood there, holding a glass in each hand as his gaze settled on the tableau. "I hope not, because it's lame." He held one of the glasses out to Cassandra. "I brought you some lemonade."

Michael had seen Cassandra the moment she entered the room. In truth, he'd been waiting for her. He'd been tainted by Hollywood parties, so he didn't enjoy them much anymore and would have made an early exit except for the possibility Cassandra would come.

Even as he conversed with one of Horty's colleagues, a professor of astronomy, he'd watched for her—he couldn't help himself.

A few minutes had gone by when he'd seen Cheryl, then Waverly confront Cassandra. He understood then this would be the one party he would not only be approaching her but rescuing her from Waverly's viciousness. He'd picked two glasses of what he'd hope was lemonade off the tray of a passing waiter before making his way over to the tense conversation on the other side of the room.

"Michael Kiley." Waverly instantly became all sweetness and light. "You came in on the wrong end of this conversation," she twittered. "Did you get my email? I didn't get my invitation to your theater opening? Everyone else on the business leaders forum received theirs."

Not looking at Waverly, he said, "I'll make sure yours is hand-delivered." His eyes were on Cassandra. "Are you hungry, Cassie?" he asked. "I asked for some lobster rolls and salad to be taken out to the gazebo for us."

"Thank you, Michael," Cassandra said, her words seeming heart-felt. "Lead the way to the gazebo."

Michael took her other hand before saying to the two other women, "Enjoy the party."

The couple strolled through the now crowded room, saying brief hello's here and there to some of the other guests, but not stopping to converse with anyone.

They almost made it out, but Abby caught them at the glass doors. "You're leaving already?"

"It's all right, Abby," Cassandra said soothingly, then continued to their destination.

Outside, they circled the pool and walked over to the small, white gazebo. Inside, a table sat between two comfortable-looking wicker chairs, a tray of the promised lobster rolls and salad waiting for them.

Cassandra put down her glass before sinking into a chair and expelling a long breath.

"You know, I've never been a fan of the roll. One of this states number one by-products. I prefer the fried clams."

"Next time," Michael said and took his seat across from her.

"I'm not really hungry anyway."

"I didn't think you were. And by the way, you look beautiful in that dress."

She smiled, feeling some of the tension from the confrontation with Waverly draining out. This man had always been able to make her feel better, special.

"You don't look half bad yourself." As a matter fact,

Michael looked gorgeous, in the simple, natural way of good genes and good health.

They sat for a while listening to the low sounds of the party far off, enjoying the coolness in their little enclosure before Michael asked, "I told you Langston was in town, right?"

"You said you'd spoken to him recently and he has a new house. How's Shauna, whom I still haven't met, and they've been together six years already—and four children … wow."

"Everyone's fine. I asked him to the party but you know how much he hates parties. The only reason he'll be at the theater's gala is because many of the folks who've bought his work will be there. Did I tell you his new house is on Shirley Street?"

"Really?" Cassandra was intrigued. "How far from the Eustis' house?"

"Not far."

Cassandra dropped back into the chair. "I always loved visiting the Eustis mansion," she said with fond memories. "I always felt just like Elizabeth Bennett whenever I strolled through those Georgian rooms."

"Well, he's just a few doors down. Remember that time Langston created our tickets for that Black Eyed Peas concert?"

"Created? How about counterfeited." She laughed at the memory. "I'll never forget it; one of the highlights of my teen years. I knew security was going to take one look at those fakes and boot us right out on our butts, then call our folks."

"Which would have been a disaster. I'm the one who'd taken my mother's car without permission." Michael suddenly grinned. "And afterwards—"

"Joy-riddin'," they said in unison and laughed.

Cassandra relaxed further back into the chair. She felt comfortable, even languorous being enclosed in this small space with Michael; he made loving him so damn easy.

"Those were some fun times," he said.

"We were together a lot," Cassandra added, "the three of us, I mean."

"Have you wondered what would have happened to us if we hadn't gone our separate ways, to carve out our own paths?" His dark gaze was penetrating as it held hers. "If we'd stayed right here in Boston—you and I—would we still be friends, you think, Cassie? Or possibly more?"

"More," she said softly, "much more." She sat forward toward him, to be closer but to also make him understand what she was feeling at this moment and how it was making her question everything about her life, herself. "I didn't come back here to change my life, but then, you come along out of the blue and turned everything upside down."

"Make it right, then by not going back and forgetting about Hollywood."

"It might have been that easy for you, Michael; it's not that easy for me. You're realizing all your ambitions, your dreams, while I'm still chasing mine."

"Stop the chase, dream about something else—us—giving us a chance."

"I wish I could, but there's something in me that can't turn away from what I've been striving for all this time, who I believe I can be, what I can achieve. I have to see it through to the end—no matter what."

"I'm not going to give up, Cassie, it's not in my nature; you know that."

She stood. "And you know," she said pointedly, "neither is it in mine."

"You going back inside?" he asked, getting to his feet.

"No way. I'm going to take my dad back his car, it's getting late."

"Let me walk you to—" Michael began.

"No." She shook her head. "I'll be fine, alone."

"There's no need to be, Cassie," he said quietly.

Stepping forward, he put his hands underneath her hair, placed his mouth against hers, causing her lips to open automatically, and kissed her deeply.

Cassandra threw her arms around him tight and let herself go into him, into his hands, the wonderful smell of him, the feel of his body so large and warm against hers, for as long as she could; she let herself ravish his mouth until they couldn't breathe.

She pulled back from him with a groan, sucking in breath. "Michael, please, you're not being fair to me, and I won't have it."

Turning quickly out of his arms, she exited their hideaway. She wanted to look back but did not and forced herself to keep going, or she'd turn right back to him.

CHAPTER THIRTEEN

The next day, Cassandra decided to do some shopping early, before the heat of the day caught her. She took an uber a few minutes before 10 a.m. to a few of her favorite shops on Winter Street in downtown Boston. She was happy to see they were still in their same location, not having migrated to the suburbs or gone out of business, unable to compete with online retailers.

She was home by eleven-forty-five and had only just set down her purse and two shopping bags filled with a green summer skirt, two tops, and a pair of dangly silver earrings, when she heard a car pull into the driveway and doors open and close.

She stepped over to the window, looked out, and pulled open the back door. Nicholas and Lexxie ran up the porch steps, almost tumbling over each other before they stopped a hairs-breath from running into her legs.

"Good morning, you animals," she said, bending and planting loud kisses on top of their sweet-smelling heads.

"We're not animals," Nicholas piped up. "We're kids."

"Kids are baby goats, so you're animals. Get in here, or should I ask in your own language?" She opened the door wide. "Baa-baa-baa."

The little ones giggled and ran inside, through the kitchen and out toward their playroom.

"Where's Mom?' Layla asked, entering behind them.

"Hello to you too, Layla." Cassie closed the door behind her sister, who she thought looked tired and drawn in the early light.

"Sorry," Layla said. "I was expecting to see Mom."

"She's upstairs. As soon as she hears the babies, she'll be down."

"Okay then." Layla sounded distracted. "I'll see her later. My water heater's busted, and I have to get a new one."

"You want me to get Dad?"

Her sister shook her head. "He deserves to rest on his first days of full retirement. And anyway, he does more than enough for us."

"Where's Alex," Cassandra asked. "On a camp-out, another drill or whatever he does."

Layla stared at her. "What's that supposed to mean?"

Cassandra, who'd picked up her shopping bags, dropped them back down onto the stool. "That he's never around."

"He's a state trooper as well as in the National Guard, Cass. So, when he's not working, he's on guard duty. He has a lot of responsibility, and it keeps him busy."

"Keeps him away, you mean. And what about his responsibility to his family, Layla?"

"You have no clue what happens around here on a daily basis with my family—anybody's family for that matter."

"I talk to Mom."

"You don't talk to me."

"Because you won't."

"What are you going to do about anything anyway? Your miles away and only deem to grace us with your exalted presence when you feel like it."

"Wait one minute." Cassandra's voice rose helplessly. "I visit as often as I can."

"Not often enough," Layla cut in. "At least I'm right here."

"By yourself, doing everything—taking care of the babies, the bills, the house while your so-called 'partner' is off—"

"Doing his job," Layla cut in.

"Then why won't he marry you, Layla?" Cassandra asked boldly, stopping her sister's next words. "Being a bride—it's all you've ever wanted since we were little. Remember when that playhouse out back was the church? Your grooms were Miller and Henry, who used to live two doors down. They would take turns from week to week being the groom. Talia and I would be the bridesmaids while Mrs. Carmody's dog, JoJo, acted as the guest.

"We had that old Diana Ross Barbie officiate as the minister, throwing our voices, shouting out the vows. We had so much fun playing out our version of the wedding ceremony at least ten times in a row every time. Now, you seem to have put away what you wanted all your life. While Alex lives out his dreams."

"Dreams." Layla almost spat out the word. "How's that going for you? Playing an extra."

"Background artist."

"I had to grow up, Cass, and put certain things away to take care of what and who I have to now."

"At least I haven't given up," Cassandra shot back.

"What in the world is going on in here?" their mother said, entering the room, a frown on her face. "You'll wake your father with your snapping at each other. What're you two arguing about?"

"I came to drop off the kids because I have to go get a new water heater, when Cass so generously tossed out her two cents on my relationship without—as usual—being asked."

"This is not the nineteenth century, Layla." Cassandra stared at her sister. "You have a life too and a right to have what you want."

The back door opened, and Talia came in followed by her best friend, Peaches. The three women were so wrapped in their own tableau they hadn't even heard her car pull into the driveway.

"What's going on?" Talia asked wide-eyed.

"Are you happy?"

"Are you?" Layla shot back.

"What about you?" Cassandra turned on Talia.

"We just stopped for coffee." Talia sounded confused.

"Shush," their mother said, the word a throwback to their childhood, and it had the same effect as it had then: they instantly shushed.

Yvonne turned to the young woman with Talia and put a friendly hand on her arm. "Nice to see you, Sophia. You can see how much the sisters missed each other," she said drily.

"Glad to see you all too in the midst of your family reunion," said Sophia Rodriguez, whom everyone called Peaches because of the dusky, warm color of her skin and the fact that when she smiled her cheeks were as round as a peach. She had been Talia's best friend since nursery school.

No one said anything into the awkward silence until Mrs. Chaletain turned to her youngest daughter. "Don't you have a water heater to buy? You'll want hot water sometime today."

"You're right," Layla said, momentarily having forgotten her errand while engaging maddingly with her sister. She turned to the door, searching through her pockets for her car keys. "I'd better go before the store gets too crowded. Tell Lexxie and Nicholas I'll be back soon."

Yvonne turned to Cassandra. "While you have to get ready for your date?"

"What date?" Cassandra asked, the three-hundred-sixty turn of conversation knocking her slightly off-balance.

Her mother pointed out the window. "He's coming into the driveway."

The four other women followed Cassandra's gaze and saw Michael pulling into the space next to Talia's car. He got out, holding a white baker's box with the word *Barronas* written on its side. They all watched him take the backstairs up to the porch. Michael, probably feeling their eyes on him, looked toward the window and waved.

"That's the guy who helped me get the presents into the car," Layla said.

"He went to school with us," Cassandra added.

"I know." Layla opened the door to ~~Michael~~ him. "Hi, Michael."

"Hello, Layla," Michael greeted her. "I hope you got all the gifts home safely."

"I did," she said, moving past him. "Bye."

He moved into the kitchen, his eyes immediately going to Cassandra.

"Good morning, Michael," Mrs. Chaletain said, "It's nice to see you again and before noon time," she said pointedly.

He held the box out to Mrs. Chaletain. "I was passing by, saw the line was ten deep instead of its usual twenty, and stopped for some rolls and tarts."

She took it and smiled politely. "This is a treat. You know Talia, of course?"

"Yep," Talia said and grabbed the box, opening it so she and Peaches could view the goodies. "Papaya tarts, still warm." She picked out a flaky pastry, handed it to Peaches before picking one out for herself and biting into it. "So good, thanks."

"Have a seat, please," Mrs. Chaletain offered. "It seems Cassie—who's usually as gregarious as the day is long—has forgotten her manners. "Would you like some coffee?"

"Oh, sorry," Cassandra finally spoke up and moved over to a cupboard for a cup. "We have pusties too from the grandparents."

"We'll have those later." Mrs. Chaletain took the baker's box from Talia. "I think I'll go check on the babies and treat them to these tarts." She looked at Talia and Peaches. "You two come along, there's enough in here for seconds."

"And maybe thirds," Talia said as she and her friend followed Mrs. Chaletain out of the room.

Cassandra poured Michael a cup of coffee and handed it

to him.

"It's okay." He sat it on the counter. "I didn't come for coffee, but to take you on a field trip, if you would like to come? Breakfast included."

She looked into his gray eyes and over the sculptured lips and smooth beard. He was wearing dark gray pants and a cerulean blue pristine shirt with the sleeves rolled up; the color and fabric hugged his athletic physique and spotlighted his handsomeness. She figured it would be hard to say no to this man, so she didn't.

"All right," she said. "I have to change clothes and will be back in a flash."

True to her word, Cassandra was back in the kitchen less than twenty minutes later, wearing her new green skirt and dangly earrings, along with a sleeveless, white silk blouse printed with tiny green flowers and completed with a wide yellow belt that accentuated her small waist and curves. She'd put her hair up in a glossy topknot, reveling her beautiful face with her wide, hazel eyes and soft lips.

"I'm going to tell Mom I'm leaving."

Cassandra walked down the hall and into the large playroom filled with toys, including a planet of LEGOs and a wall of books Nicholas and Lexxie seemed to never get tired of being read from. Her mother sat at the play table reading to Lexxie and Nicholas, *I Am Enough* by Grace Byers, the two absorbed by the story.

"Mom, I'm going now."

They all looked up at her.

"You look pretty, Aunty Cassie," said Nicholas.

"I like your earrings," said Lexxie.

"Thanks for the compliments, you animals," Cassandra said, and the children burst into giggles before getting up and running over to pick up Barbie dolls.

"I really didn't mean to upset her," she said.

Her mother nodded, understanding. "Some things you have to keep to yourself, Cassie."

"But I want to help her, see her happy."

"You can't 'will' someone to be happy"—her mother's tone was patient—"especially when you don't know what's going on in their lives—even the lives of your sisters."

"You're right. I'll try and keep my opinion to myself and my mouth closed."

"You're too much like me"—her mother smiled—"so I don't believe that'll fly for long."

LORELEI HENDERSON

CHAPTER FOURTEEN

Finally leaving the house, Cassandra got into the car with Michael and settled herself. "Where are we going for breakfast? I really don't care. I had one pastry today, and I'm so hungry, a McDonald's McMuffin will do."

"I believe I can do better than that," Michael said.

They drove out of Boston and headed onto the freeway, the car eating up the miles. Cassandra opened the window and let the breeze ride with them.

"Your sisters are great—your entire family is," Michael said, maneuvering the car expertly through the streets.

Cassandra laughed. "You only met them a couple of times."

"I've known you for a long time, so I had an inkling they would be great too."

"Michael, you're too nice for your own good," she said and felt a bright blush heat her skin. This man could stir her emotions like no one else.

"I'm envious, that's all, having no siblings of my own—good or bad, irritating or ridiculous."

"Irritating describes them perfectly. You have no relatives in the city? I remember once seeing your mother at a school function."

"She's been gone for two years now. I have a second cousin in Delaware and a grandfather who lives in

Somerset."

Michael's last words piqued her interest, most people said "my grandfather," while he'd said, "a grandfather." She wondered instantly what was going on there.

After a while, small cities and towns they passed became rural townships and farming villages. At one of these villages, Michael headed the car down a road that was green on both sides with a variety of crops. He then turned off onto a long-graveled lane, which made Cassandra take extra notice. Beyond the lane she could see rolling green hills and thick, forested trees. At one point she saw a man walking a cluster of sheep.

"Where are we?" she asked without looking around at Michael, her gaze steady on the verdant scenery around them.

"I told you my grandfather was the manager of a farm, and this is it; it's called Grand Nelsan. "

"A bed-and-breakfast." Cassandra saw from the sign positioned near the lane that read: *Grand Nelsan Bed-and-Breakfast*. At the sight of the house they were headed for, she caught her breath. "It's right out of *Pride and Prejudice*. A castle."

It wasn't as large as a castle, yet it was big and two-storied, a Tudor country house made of golden-yellow stone. It had a curved, sandstone driveway out front and in its center sat a small, flowing fountain surrounded by flowers. Michael drove the car around the drive and parked off to one side. They watched couples and other people stroll and bicycle around the house and the grounds.

"My grandfather, Nelsan, was the manager of this place. It started out as an organic farm-cooperative, that prided itself on sustainable farming; all owned unsurprisingly—maybe even a little unjustly—by my father's father. My grandparents, Nelsan and Francis lived here; it was where my mother grew up. My grandmother died when my Mom was nine.

"And when my grandfather Nelsan died, the farm

started to go downhill and my father's dad could care less; he was on the verge of selling all twenty acres when I bought it from him. I had no idea how to run a farm, and a friend suggested I add to it instead of tearing it to small parcels or just letting it sit. And the bed-and-breakfast was born; that was eight years ago, and to my surprise, it does well."

"Come on," Cassandra said eagerly, throwing the door open and getting out. "I have to see the rest."

Michael followed suit and had turned toward the house when Cassandra stopped him.

"I want to look around the outside first—I always look at the grounds first if I can."

"No problem." Michael extended his arm, and Cassandra hooked hers through his. "Let's stroll."

Without speaking, they walked out toward a pasture with rolling hills far off, half of it covered in trees. On one of the hills stood the man with the sheep they'd seen earlier. A fluffy dog sat at his feet as they watched the small group of grazing animals. It was the epitome of bucolic life.

They walked down a lane to a pond, where at one end, a small bridge crossed. On the other side was a rock wall, and beyond that, more bright, green pasture. It seemed as if a piece of the English countryside had been dropped right in this New England spot.

Cassandra gazed at the pond, the bulrushes in the water swayed, flowers jutted around the water's edge as bees buzzed and other insects whirled around. The sun sparkled off the water and caused the entire place to be surrounded by a drowsy, other-worldly haze; it was a romance lover's dream come true.

"It's serene, almost magical," Cassandra said.

"This was my mother's favorite place. She told me once how she'd come here to think, to get away from it all; when her life hung heavy."

Cassandra nodded, understanding that feeling well. Michael's mother sounded like a person she would have liked very much.

"You hungry yet?" Michael asked.

"Yes," Cassandra said and sighed. She was reluctant to leave this spot, but she did want to see the "manor house." "What's in the rear of the castle?"

"Not a castle. A good-sized stone house."

"How many rooms?" she asked as they walked slowly back the way they'd come.

"Ten guest rooms with en suite baths. We can take a tour later if you want."

As they rounded the side of the house, Cassandra ran her hand over the cool, yellow stone. In the back sat garden tables and chairs outside a set of glass double doors that looked into a small dining room. An actual flower garden was a few feet away, and beyond that stretched perfect green lawns.

There were several doors that led into the house, and Michael opened one, letting her proceed him inside. Cassandra found herself in a large kitchen so big it boasted a walk-in fire-place. Three women stood in front of two ranges while a man stood setting out large bowls of sugar, eggs, and flour onto a square wooden table that could have seated fourteen people.

The four people looked up as the door opened, and at the sight of Michael right behind her, they immediately dropped what they were doing and came forward with smiles wreathing their faces.

"Mikey," one of the ladies called, her wide, brown eyes full of welcome as she embraced him in thick arms. "So glad to see you; it's been weeks. We were just talking about you yesterday, weren't we, Sylvia?"

"Yes, we were, Patty," said the curly- and gray-haired woman, her thin features solemn except for her eyes, which were dark and gleamed with kindness. She put her hands on her small hips. "You must be hungry. Both of you," she said in greeting.

"This is Cassandra," Michael addressed the curly-haired woman. "This is Sylvia, and that's Patty."

"Hi, everybody," Cassandra said, "I'm definitely hungry."

"We're practically dropping with hunger, Patty." He glanced at the other two people in the room. "Hi, Denise, Ramon."

"Nice to see you, Michael," said Ramon while Denise gave Michael a wave from where she stood over a huge boiling pot of broth at one of the stoves.

"So, let us get you settled then," Sylvia said briskly, then, "Patty."

Patty turned and walked into a pantry Cassandra hadn't noticed and came back out with a stack of plates, cups, bowls, and silverware in her arms.

"Let's seat you two in the warm alcove." Patty winked. "Follow me."

The two followed and the alcove turned out to be a private nook the size of a small study surrounded by windows. The nook held a plain table with a tablecloth that featured cornucopias and two wooden chairs made comfortable by thick, red seat cushions. The windows were covered in white birdsong lace that at once gave an air of privacy while simultaneously allowing for looking out and watching the world go by. Cassandra saw that it was an intimate hideaway in plain sight.

Patty set the table with the dining ware, then stepped back. "We're gonna get started," she said, and left for the kitchen side.

"Get started?" Cassandra asked, looking curiously at Michael.

He shrugged. "They don't see me often enough, and when they do, they think I'm starving and need to fatten me up. So, get ready," he warned.

They heard the clatter of pots and pans, heard then smelled frying bacon and sausages. Denise appeared, smiling shyly and looking all of seventeen, holding a tray with glasses of water, orange juice, tomato juice, and fruit juice, plus a large bowl of fresh fruit. Michael stood and took the tray, settling it onto the table.

"Thank you, Denise."

The girl nodded, a blush hitting her cheeks before she disappeared back around the corner. The delicious smell of baking biscuits suddenly wafted toward them. Cassandra placed bowls of fruit in front of Michael, then herself.

"There's fruit trees on the property," he said.

Cassandra picked up a large strawberry and bit into it, finding it juicy and exceptionally sweet. "This is so good."

The two ate the fruit in silence, savoring the fresh taste. Cassandra looked over her shoulder when she heard an approaching cart. It was Sylvia this time, and the cart was laden down with breakfast food; everything Cassandra could imagine. Michael watched her with serious indulgence.

"We can't possibly eat all of this," she stage whispered, her eyes almost unable to take in the array of food on offer.

"We're only supposed to try," Michael whispered back.

As Sylvia stopped beside them, he stood and helped her place as many dishes on the tabletop as it could hold. The dishes included scrambled eggs, boiled eggs, egg almandine, bacon, sausage, Canadian ham, hash browns, waffles, French toast, cinnamon rolls, Texas toast, jams, jellies, creamy butter, and various marmalades.

"I'll tell you now," Cassandra began, overwhelmed, "my eyes are bigger than my stomach. I won't be able to get more than ten bites out of any of this."

"Don't worry, Cassie; none of it will go to waste, I promise. We try and use everything we grow, make or barter around here."

Sylvia handed Cassandra two freshly laundered and perfectly folded linen napkins before departing with the cart. Over their gastronomic feast, the two dug in as much as they could while they talked between bites of the great tasting fare.

"You remember Ms. Radcliffe?" Michael asked, spooning a couple more strawberries onto Cassandra's plate.

"I do." The woman's image popped into her head, making her smile. "She had those eyebrows that made her look like Faye Dunaway in *Mommy Dearest*."

"Yes, and she could speak entire sentences with those brows."

They both laughed at the shared experience.

"Remember when she told us Radcliffe College had been named after her family?" Cassandra asked.

"I worked in the office," Michael said, "and found out her last name came from her family all right; they owned a beer hall and sandwich shop in Weymouth."

"No," Cassandra said in pretend shock before they both broke up into laughter again like naughty school children. "Michael, you worked in the office, on the school newspaper, and in the drama department as director, writer, acting coach, script supervisor—you were the epitome of the involved high school student."

"In the drama department I was the epitome all right … of a scene painter and stagehand, that was about it. You, though, were truly involved, Cassie. You acted, sang, and you rewrote many of the scripts, made them ten times better so that the kids loved playing those scenes. Do you still write?"

Cassandra shrugged. "Now and then short pieces and audition monologues for my friends—nothing big deal."

"I'm sure they're a big deal. The plays and shows you wrote were terrific."

"Your memory's faulty," she quickly changed the subject and came up with the only thing that popped into her head: the weather. "I'm grateful the heat has trended down. This place is unbearable when it gets over seventy-five degrees; the same as when it's under twenty-five."

"I'm glad it's cooled down too if it makes you enjoy being home."

She smiled. "It's been a long time since I've called this town home."

"But it is," Michael said, unsmiling now, "because it's where your family loves you."

"Maybe so, but winters here?" She shivered in mock fright. "I couldn't take them anymore. How do you do it, Michael? Especially having lived in California with the year-round sunshine."

"I'll tell you a secret …" He lowered his voice. "Well, maybe not a secret: I don't stay around all winter, sometimes not at all. I have a house in Sarasota, a quiet little enclave, Stephen King's my neighbor."

"You're kidding?" she said, slightly awed. "He's got more movies going than any other Hollywood writer in years."

"Not at all. I walk the beach a lot when I'm there and so does he, and when we run across each other, he always has time for an interesting conversation."

So taken with each other; time seemed to fly by as they paid more attention to each other than the food in front of them. When they could eat no more, Michael went for the cart and they piled the untouched food neatly on its shelves and wheeled it all back to the kitchen, where the women put the food on warming plates.

Michael picked up a wall phone and spoke into the mouthpiece, "Hey, Sebastian, this is Michael." He listened. "Fine, how about you? How's Isadore? … Good, tell her hello, from me. Listen, there's tons of food ready to eat over here. Bring your crew for a meal and anyone else you find along the way." He listened again. "Good, I'll see you on my next visit."

As Cassandra stood listening, she noticed Sylvia, Patty, and Ramon whispering and looking at her. She figured it couldn't be because they'd seen her in something, so she walked over and joined them.

"Who's Sebastian?" she asked.

"He's one of our two farm managers. The place has gotten so big, it needs two people to oversee it," Ramon said.

"The other's Gary, and he's in Connecticut, at Yale University taking a class in tree conservation," Sylvia said, then looked with unbidden curiosity at Cassandra. "Who're you?"

"A friend of Michael's."

"A friend?" Ramon asked, then glanced at Patty, who raised an eyebrow at him.

"What?" Cassandra knew she was missing something and needed them to clarify her suspicion. "You've never met a friend of Michael's?"

"Never," Patty spoke up.

"Michael's never, ever brought a friend here or anybody else. I mean, Mr. Demarion and his family visit all the time because they're practically family. But never a friend."

"Especially a girlfriend," Ramon said, grinning.

"Oh," was all Cassandra said, suddenly nonplussed by what their curiosity meant, by what her entire visit might mean to them. "I'm more of the 'friend' part."

"Are you sure?" Patty asked as Denise shook her head.

Michael suddenly appeared beside Cassandra. "Ready for a tour of the house?"

She nodded. "Nice to meet you all," she addressed the three. "The breakfast was the best I'd had in a long time."

"You're welcome," Patty smiled.

"Anytime," Sylvia said.

"See you the next time," Ramon called.

Denise waived.

After they'd left the kitchen, Cassandra realized those folks in there loved Michael. Here he was holding on to his legacy, which wasn't only the buildings or the farm land, but the people who called this place home. The thing was, she loved him too and had thought about asking him to come with her back to California. But being here and meeting Sylvia, Patty, and the others; she knew she couldn't do it. Michael belonged here, in this part of the world, and she belonged in hers.

CHAPTER FIFTEEN

Michael and Cassandra exited the kitchen, down a long hallway, and threw a door.

"This is one way from the main kitchen to the main part of the house."

They went up a small set of stairs that ended at a door he pushed open, allowing her to proceed him. Cassandra found herself in a carpeted, circular grand entrance hall with a small discreet desk and chair to one side. In the center of the entry hall was a beautiful mahogany table with a circle of flower vases in different colors and shapes and made of various materials: porcelain, glass, crystal and all filled with a variety of fresh flowers. Off to the side was a lavish, rose-carpeted main staircase, its banister gleamed of wood and brass. Light poured down the stairwell and Cassandra peered up and saw a glass cupola.

Michael then led her to a room on the right, and Cassandra peered into a formal dining room, next to it was a formal living room with a huge fireplace surrounded by restful sofas and chairs. A grand piano sat in one corner of the room and in another, a table and chairs for an intimate conversation or a friendly card game. On the walls were landscape and sea paintings, the scenes appealing while being nostalgic at the same time.

He showed her a formal lounge and two smaller ones.

There was a library stuffed with books of all kinds that would fit anyone's taste, shelves of knick-knacks Cassandra decided was a very British-country-manor house touch along with comfortable chairs and a blue loveseat. In this room, she walked around looking at the books and touching the knacks she thought cute or funny. She stopped at a shelf in the corner where among the knicks was a small picture of a family: a mother, father, and baby. The mother was African American and the father Caucasian. The two held the baby boy lovingly between them, and all were smiling.

"You and your parents," she stated.

Michael nodded. "We didn't take many pictures together, and that's one of maybe three."

Cassandra kept her eyes on the photograph. "Your family, and now they're gone."

Michael didn't comment, only asked, "Are you done with the tour? I have another surprise for you."

"No, I want to see all of it."

"All right, it's only a few more rooms to see on this floor."

He showed her a sitting room, a bar, and a game room.

"There are six bedrooms on the second level and four on the third, a little smaller but still nice."

"I have no doubt about that," Cassandra said, impressed by everything she'd seen so far.

"I'll show you around upstairs."

They climbed the elaborate staircase onto a circular landing with rooms on all sides. Cassandra noticed a second, narrower staircase on the left.

"Are all the rooms booked?"

"Yes, for the rest of the summer from what Sylvia told me. There is one bedroom I can show you; the guest won't be here until the afternoon."

Michael pushed a door open on the left, and Cassandra walked inside. It was a lovely room with gleaming wooden floors covered by a brightly colored tasseled rug. A large four-poster bed sat in the middle of the floor. There was a walk-in wardrobe and two comfortable chairs in front of a fireplace. Cassandra walked over to the windows, which looked out onto woodland.

"Thank you for bringing me here, Michael. I wouldn't have missed coming here for anything.

He walked over and gently took her face between his hands. "Seeing you here, I'll never see it again without you in it."

It sounded sweet and sad at the same time and echoed her earlier thoughts, and because of that, Cassandra kissed him to make them both feel better.

A little while later, they left Grand Nelsan with Cassandra helplessly looking back, determined never to forget the place.

A few miles outside of Boston, Michael said, "I have to stop at the theater for a few minutes to sign a few papers, if you don't mind; it won't take too long. Then onto the second stop on our field trip."

"I don't mind," Cassandra said. "I didn't see nearly enough of it on my first visit." She was eager to explore the theater some more, the same as she'd done at Grand Nelsan.

When they pulled into the staff parking lot, Michael said, "You can come up to the office if you like or wander around anywhere to your heart's content."

"I'll wander," she said.

"When you're done, my office is on the third floor; anyone around can direct you to me."

"Okay, and your papers are calling."

With a squeeze of her hand, he walked inside. Cassandra decided to start on the outside of the theater and work her way into its interior. Making her way around the side of the building, she took in its design, noticing how the combination of strategically placed metal panels, the sandy color of the brick along with the placement of the windows—some jutting off in various angles—that the theater was designed like a sunburst and was positioned right in the heart of Roxbury so that everything great and wonderful revolved around it just as the planets revolved around the sun.

She noticed lights housed underneath the windows and imagined them lit at night; they would light up the theater like a nova. Michael's architect friend was truly gifted. She walked for a few minutes more until she came to a large spot of rich, black, furrowed soil, and stopped.

Moving through the dirt, turning over the soil with a booted foot as if he were a farmer in a field, was a man, wearing khaki pants, a blue work shirt, and a straw hat. As she watched, he took off the hat, and Cassandra stared. Was that the actor Brian White who had actually been in a movie with Taraji P Henson? No, it couldn't be, she told herself, no way. What would he be doing here looking at dirt?

He looked up, saw her there, waved, then hurried toward her. Startled, she stepped back, meaning to go back the way she'd come.

"Hi, Cassie," he said. "Or should I call you Cassandra? I recognized you immediately."

She stared at him. "I'm sorry, I don't think I know you."

He grinned at her and stuck out a gloved hand. "Sorry." He quickly took off the glove and stuck his hand out again. "I'm Demarion Asher."

"You designed this building," she said and took his hand, giving it a quick shake. "It's beautiful, and it belongs."

"That's the best compliment an architect can receive," he said. "I'm glad to finally meet you. I used to think you'd never make it back here, which would have been a real shame the way Michael feels about you. You going into the theater?"

"Yes," Cassandra said and started off again.

"Great, I'm going that way too, mind if I tag along with you?" He matched her pace. "Michael has been talking about you for … forever."

Cassandra felt a flush of pleasure mixed with

embarrassment as he went on. "I was just checking out the surroundings before going inside."

"No problem, I'll walk with you," he said and joined her. "We wanted this place to fit the neighborhood, its essence, as if it had grown right out of the soil."

"It definitely has an organic flavor," Cassandra said, again admiring the joined brick and metal that came together seamlessly.

"A neighborhood feel you think?"

"Absolutely," Cassandra said, and they smiled at each other.

On first impression, Cassandra decided she liked this man.

"What were you doing back there in the dirt?" she suddenly asked as they approached the front entrance.

"Grass seeds were recently planted in that spot," Demarion said proudly. "Next year, it'll be a sea of green bordered by tulips, though I was thinking zinnias because they take less water."

"So, you're not only an architect, Demarion, but a gentleman farmer too."

"Please call me, Dee. Hannah, my wife—she'll like you by the way—says that I'd hot foot her and the kids to Kansas for land and a tractor if it was on offer, and she's right."

They stopped at the building's front entrance, and he opened one of the doors for her.

"Cassie, it was terrific finally meeting you, " he said. "Now, it's my duty to give Michael a hard time about it."

"Please don't. I'd hate to embarrass him."

"He can take it." He smiled briefly, then sobered as he gazed directly into her eyes. "Michael's the real deal, you know, a knight in shining armor; you can see that in what he's done for Roxbury, can't you? He'll do anything for those he loves; it's the way he's made. Yet, anyone can be hurt; especially by those whom we love the most."

Cassandra didn't retreat from his gaze, her own was

steady. "Why are you telling me this?"

"Maybe because it needs to be said, and I figured Michael wouldn't."

"Why would he need to?" she asked, taken aback. "I would never do anything to hurt, Michael."

"Maybe not intentionally."

"Not at all," she said decisively.

Demarion's phone rang, breaking their conversation. He took it out of a pocket and looked at it. "Excuse me a minute," he said to Cassandra.

"No need, I'll continue my tour." She stepped into the theater's foyer, where tourists and sight-seers milled around.

"I'm sure we'll see each other again," he called after her before walking away to speak into the phone.

Cassandra frowned as her second impression of Mr. Archer went south. She didn't want to hurt Michael deliberately, knowing that her leaving would do just that. Her only consolation was that she'd be in living with that same pain, knowing they'd never be together again.

It took her a few seconds to realize that the people who'd been milling about in the lobby had all suddenly started up the stairs toward the theater proper. She wondered about it until she heard it: singing. Wonderful singing.

She followed up the staircase and into the main auditorium, where people sat helter-skelter, staring down at the warmly lit stage, where a group of people was obviously rehearsing a scene from a play. To the right of them a young man sat at a grand piano, his fingers on the keys. At center stage was a young woman standing silently, her hands folded in front of her chest.

As they watched, she breathed in once, then out, and began singing—without accompaniment—in a voice that rang with such pure and clear resonance. Cassandra sank down in one of the seats without her realizing it, captivated by the sound. It filled the hall with such radiance, a gift of perfect pitch. Cassandra hadn't been dazzled by so vibrant a voice since she'd been lucky enough to attend a concert by Audra McDonald.

The young woman suddenly stopped singing, struck a poise, and started talking, "So, the day after I turned eighteen …"

Cassandra instantly recognized it as Val's monologue from the musical *A Chorus Line*. As she watched, the actor spoke with her entire body, her face, her hands, even her hair. Cassandra was mesmerized and by the looks on the faces of everyone else in the theater; they felt the same. They, as any audience should be, were in her power. She was electric and held them in the palm of her hand, gripped by her incredible, natural talent.

Cassandra was no exception. She sat until the monologue was done, and while everyone else was clapping, she exited the theater. She knew then that she not only wasn't a good actor, she was also a fool for kidding herself all these years in believing she had talent. She'd lived a lie of her own dreams and desires, and they'd just come crashing in on her.

CHAPTER SIXTEEN

Michael found her a few minutes later leaning against his car, staring out into space. He looked at her and knew instantly something had happened.

"What's wrong?" he asked. "Here, let's get into the car and out of the heat." He opened the car door, saw her inside before going around to his, and starting the engine, letting the cool air flow. "Cassie, what happened?"

She hadn't said a word, and he was alarmed by the blank look on her face.

"She was so good," Cassandra said, sounding stunned.

"Who?"

"The actor rehearsing on the stage. No, she wasn't just good, she enthralled everyone in the room, including me, with her skill, her presence. Michael." She finally looked at him, a ripple of devastation in her gaze. "I realized in that moment: I'll never be that good—even half that good. I don't have what she has, 'it,' and no matter how many classes I take, auditions I go on, or commercials I book … it's just not in me."

"That's not true."

"Yes, it is, and I need to accept it."

"No, you don't," he stated emphatically, willing to do anything to ease the hurt he saw on her face. "Let me show you how talented you are."

***

Michael drove them away from the Roxbury Community Theater and down streets and into neighborhoods, Casandra had always been eager to put into her rearview mirror. She gazed out the window at the passing shops, office complexes, and triple-decker houses. This part of town hadn't changed much except for new coats of paint here and there or the change from a bodega to a coffee house. Everything else was the same, and for once, she wasn't sure that was a bad thing.

She, even now feeling reluctant to admit it, did love this town despite its traumatic history of racial intolerance and violence, its crowded classism, and even its sometimes-intolerable weather. She had to love it because it was as Michael said: those whom she loved most in the world were right here.

"Where are we going again?"

"I didn't say, but we're not far; as a matter of fact, it's coming up." He turned a corner. "In a minute you'll have some idea."

"This is the way to …" She broke off when she recognized Mulder Street and a few minutes later down the block, their former high school. "What's going on?"

"You'll see," Michael said with a brief smile.

He drove round to the back of the large school and parked.

"Hey, they put up a new science wing." Cassandra gestured toward a large, glass-fronted building that had two swooping, curving sides, reminding her of a woman's slender, arched neck. "It's beautiful, like something that should be sitting on the campus of MIT."

"It was a design by Frank Gehry."

"What are those cursive dangling letters? They look like dangly earrings."

"They stand for the chemical elements."

They got out of the car and walked up to a set of steel double doors. Cassandra noticed that behind what looked like bulletproof glass, was a set of cameras. Beside the door was an intercom, and Michael pressed the button. A few seconds later, a disembodied voice answered.

"Roxbury High School, can I help you?"

"Hello, this is Michael Kiley, I have a meeting in the theater department."

"We have you on the guest list."

"Great, and I'm here with a guest … Cassandra Chaletain."

There was an immediate buzz and a clunk, unlocking the door.

Michael pulled it open, and they entered a wide hall.

The smell hit her first, a combination of perfume, disinfectant, and high-flying hormones.

"High school." She sighed.

A number of students moved back and forth, laughing, talking, entering and exiting classrooms on each side of the vast hallway. A young man in a security uniform and wearing a heavily laden equipment belt approached them down the long hall.

"Hi, Michael."

"Hey, Tony; this is Cassandra."

"Hi," Cassandra said.

Robert stared at her for a few seconds before he finally spoke. "Nice to meet you, Ms. Cassandra. The students are in the theater," Robert said and started off the way he'd come, with them following behind.

Cassandra stared around at the place where she'd spent four long years; it was the same yet different. For one thing, everything was smaller, or so it seemed to her, and for another, every student seemed extremely young, no older than babies. She felt as if they shouldn't be allowed to be here testing the real world, but cloistered somewhere safe until the world changed for the better.

They passed long lines of classrooms filled with talking

children and faculty before rounding a corner into a wider hall. At the end of this passage stood double wooden doors, above the doors etched in the school's colors, yellow and black, were the words *Martin and Malcom Forever Auditorium*.

Robert pulled open one of the doors, and the sound of singing and chatter wafted out. They stepped inside and looked down toward the stage, where there had to be more than fifty people milling about. A group of teenagers stood around a piano as one of them played a song Cassandra recognized, "Popular" from the play *Wicked*. They all sang, not missing a word or a beat.

Cassandra was instantly taken by the scene, by the camaraderie, the acceptance, the happiness that is the hallmark of being part of the school's theater scene, if one is lucky, and she willingly, gladly gravitated toward it. She walked down the nearest aisle and sat a few rows back from the stage, taking in the organized chaos in front of her as Michael joined her.

"They're going to do *Wicked* this year?" she asked, raising her voice a bit over the commotion.

Michael nodded. "This is the second day of auditions, I think. Cassandra." He said her name in a way that left her no choice but to pull her gaze from what was happening on the stage and look at him. "I didn't just bring you here because I thought you'd enjoy visiting this place. I brought you here because I wanted you to see—well, hear—something."

"What?" she asked, genuinely puzzled.

"One second." Michael got up and walked down to the stage, where he tapped the shoulder of a man trying to wrangle in a group of teenagers who were excitedly talking as they removed violins, flutes, and trumpets from their cases.

The man turned, saw who it was, and grinned hugely as he patted Michael warmly on the arm. Michael spoke, the man nodded, and they proceeded back up the aisle to where Cassandra waited.

"Cassandra, this is Jim," Michael introduced. "The school's do-it-all director."

"No, I have tons of help from the stu …" He broke off and stared at her. Jim was a medium-sized man, wearing thick, steel-wire-rimmed glasses on a pleasant face that arranged itself into a wide smile. "Cassandra Chaletain?"

She nodded, totally nonplussed at the fact that this man—whom she didn't remember from high school all those years ago—knew her. Could he have recognized her from television or movies? Possible but not probable, she decided.

"I'm sorry, how do you know me?"

"Show her, Jim." Michael grinned.

"Gladly," Jim said, suddenly sounding excited. "You don't know how great it is to meet you. Please, follow me down; the kids will be thrilled you're here."

Confused about what was going on but willing to find out, they followed Jim to where a group of young women stood on the stage rehearsing a scene.

"Leslie," Jim called up to one of the young women, her long braids swaying in youthful exuberance. "Could you recite your creed?"

"No problem." She smiled, her dark eyes alight in her creamy, brown-skinned face. She moved closer to the center of the stage, her manner settling as she spoke clearly and directly, her voice carrying distinctly. "We recite this in the dressing room before we go on. I personally speak it as a mantra sometimes before I go to school, or if I have to speak in front of a group, even before a Spanish exam—it gives me confidence." "Here goes." Her voice rose slightly. "I believe in the wonder of myself, as the only me." Her words resonated with purpose and were filled with hope, causing the other children to quiet down and watch her perform. "My strength, my faith comes from the bottom of me, up through me to my heart, where it resounds as a wave without boundaries. To be me is to be present, loving, accepting, and to try as the goal—always the goal—to know

I can—I can do it."

Cassandra's hand had gone to her mouth in shocked disbelief as she heard out loud those words she'd written all those years ago. Now, a new generation was taking heart from them: her words. She turned and hurried, almost running, up the aisle.

"Cassie," she heard behind her but didn't stop.

She passed through the halls and banged out the doors onto the campus. Michael caught up with her as she strolled through the elements that dangled from the side of the science building; they swung lightly and chimed prettily in the gently breeze.

"These are pretty and tough," she said, "you can't pull them down."

"You're the same."

She didn't answer, and instead walked over to a covered lunch table and sat down. "I was surprised ... No, that's a lie. I was floored by Leslie's speech. Those were my words; I hadn't heard them in so long."

"It's a beautiful creed, Cassie. The first time I heard it, I knew you'd written them."

Someone called Michael's name, interrupting their moment. They turned and saw Jim hurrying toward them.

"I'm glad you're still here. Principal Nuñez asks if you'll come back in and meet with him for a minute, Michael. I'll be happy to wait here with, Cassandra."

"All right," Michael said and turned to her.

"I'm fine, you go meet."

As Michael moved off, Jim said, "It's good you've come back."

"A visit," she corrected him. "It's Michael who's back to stay."

"And we're unbelievably grateful." Jim's words sounded heartfelt. "His foundation has given generously to our theater department, plus helping get the funding to build the science center. He's a stalwart in this community, a true believer in its promise and its future."

Cassandra only nodded. She watched Jim talk animatedly with a couple of students on their way to class as they waited for Michael who joined them ten minutes later.

"See you at the party," Jim said, shaking Michael's hand, then to Cassandra, "It was wonderful to finally meet you, and not only for the students. We all love your work."

Jim walked back inside as Michael sat down beside her. They were silent for a few seconds, watching the students busily going in and out of the buildings, playing and joking around each other, enjoying the day.

"I can't believe how—"

"—much they loved—"

They spoke simultaneously, broke off, and smiled as they looked into each other's eyes. Michael took her hand. "You go."

"I don't know what to say."

"It's okay; I only wanted you to see how you're part of something. Those plays, those wonderful vignettes you wrote back then? The kids love them; they use them now as rehearsal tools, exercises, and encouragement. Your lines, when they become the spoken word, they touch people; they make them laugh; they make them happy. They believe in you, and so do I."

Cassandra's eyes closed, and her head drooped as tears she couldn't stop slid down her cheeks. He gently touched her face and wiped them away. The feel of Michael's strong fingers, the warm smoothness of his touch, made her catch her breath as her skin tingled, and without realizing she was going to do it—she threw her arms around him and hugged him close.

"Thank you," she whispered against his neck.

"Thank you back," he whispered in return. "Hey"—he pulled back—"how about some ice cream and a walk in the park?"

True to his word, thirty minutes later, they pulled into a

parking garage not too far from the Public Garden. Not long after, they strolled through one of the most famous parks in the country. As they walked without speaking though occasionally brushing shoulders, Cassandra realized two things simultaneously: she hadn't visited the park since she was Lexxie's age (had almost forgotten it even existed), and that it was truly a beautiful place.

There was the verdant green of the trees, the slow sway of the hanging Spanish moss, the greenish-blue lagoon, and flowers as far as the eyes could see. They passed countless tourists but were not overwhelmed by them as they strolled between the common and the garden.

"How about a tofu ice cream cone?" Michael asked.

Cassandra made a face of true disgust. "That's about the same as asking if I want an ant-covered hotdog."

He laughed. "It's dairy and gluten-free, vegan, and absolutely delicious." He took her hand. "Come on, Cassie, you won't regret it."

"I am not so sure."

They walked down a path where benches sat, and upon them, people eating ice cream. Up ahead of them, on the right side of the path, sat a yellow food truck with the words *We All Scream for Ice Cream* written on its side in rainbow-colored lettering. A sandwich board sat beside the truck with a list of choices. The truck's side window was open as three workers served a line of people snaking out in front.

As they walked up, one of the servers, a pretty woman with dark streaked-blond-hair tied in a ponytail saw them and called, "Hi, Michael, just a minute."

She handed the man in front of her a cone with a triple scoop of pink, blue, and yellow ice cream on top, before exiting the truck. She walked up to them, a smile on her face Cassandra saw was only for Michael. "I didn't know you were stopping by today," she said, her eyes avidly roving over his face.

"Hi, Siobhan. I wanted Cassandra to try your ice cream. I told her how good it is."

"Hello," Cassandra said and thought Siobhan looked at Michael as if he were the world's best ice cream.

"Hi." Siobhan glanced a moment at Cassandra before her eyes fell on Michael again and stayed there, starry-eyed and focused with feeling. "We can hardly get through the day without selling out."

"I'm glad to hear it's going so well."

"What would you like to try? We restocked ten minutes ago."

"We'll check the board," Michael said, then took Cassandra's hand again.

Cassandra saw Siobhan take notice of the gesture.

"When you're ready, let me know, and I'll get it for you."

"Thanks, Siobhan, and nice to see you again."

He turned them toward the sandwich board offerings as Siobhan went back inside the truck. When it was their turn, Cassandra ordered a peach ice-cream cone while Michael chose one called yellow, cherry twist.

Once they had their cones, they found an empty park bench not far from the truck and sat down.

"Go ahead," Michael urged Cassandra as he licked his cone. "Give it a try, Cassie; it won't taste anywhere near an ant-coated hot-dog."

Having always thought herself a brave sort, Cassandra stuck out her tongue and tasted the peach; to her surprise, it tasted good.

"It does taste the same as regular ice cream," she said at Michael's grin and took another lick. "Even better than that served at Jack's Place," she mentioned a favorite Venice Beach hang-out Michael would know, right on the boardwalk.

"It's better than Jack's, whose gelato I once believed had no rivals in the world." He gestured with his chin toward the ice-cream truck. "Andrew will be moving his business into the Roxbury Plaza."

"I remember, we passed it on the way to the high school," Cassandra said. "It's going to give Copley Plaza a run for its money."

Having had enough ice-cream talk, Cassandra steered the conversation to one she was more interested in exploring. "Siobhan's in love with you, by the way."

Michael stopped eating and stared at her. "No way. Why would she be?"

"You ever take her out?" Cassandra asked, narrowing in on her suspicions.

"Not really, I mean … a couple of dates and that was it."

"That's what I thought …" Cassandra was suddenly done with her ice cream. She dumped the cone in the nearest trash can with a small show of force spurned in her by a stab of jealousy she couldn't help feeling, though she knew she had no right.

"It was only two dinners, in separate cars, and it went nowhere. We both knew it wouldn't almost immediately, and we never went out again."

"That didn't stop her from falling in love with you."

"That's impossible." Michael sounded genuinely taken aback as he tossed the rest of his cone into the garbage can. "I didn't encourage her. We get along, but that's it."

Cassandra laughed. "How many times have not encouraging love prevented it from happening? Probably none; it's a force all in its own."

"There's been no one for more than two years—no one serious."

"Why not?" she asked, avidly interested in his answer.

He shrugged. "Work, projects, work, time, disinterest—any and all excuses." He looked at her. "What about you? When I saw you at those parties, you weren't alone. Hovering at your elbow had been a Brad-Pitt-look-alike."

"That was Josh," she said fondly.

***

"Was or is?" Michael asked, feeling a hot stab of jealousy. When he'd seen them together, they'd looked the

142

perfect couple, happy, carefree and the envy he'd felt of the Brad-Pitt-look-alike had been bitter.

"Was. Definitely was. All right," she began, "Now that you've done one of the nicest things for me ever." She briefly touched one of his hands. "You deserve something too."

"No, it was for you. I'm not looking for any kind of give back."

"I know you don't, but hear me out. Call your grandfather, or go see him." She watched his face close up. "You're the one who said I'm here because folks who love me are here; it's the same for you. He's not that far away, and he'll be so glad to see you."

Michael turned aside from her and looked toward the lagoon with its sailing swans. "You don't know how he is."

"No, but he's your closest relative, especially if you want to look at it literally in distance; Somerset is no more than twenty-five miles away."

Michael didn't say anything, though his mind was saying a full-stop: no.

"Your family's different from mine—yours is amazing; they're loving, kind, good people. I can feel how much you mean to each other."

"Now, I feel badly for thinking how nosey and cussed they are."

Michael laughed briefly, then said, "It's funny how having siblings can make all the difference in the world."

"For good or bad. Your parents didn't want more children?"

"I was a surprise—loved—but a surprise, though I wished mightily for siblings, of course, but my parents' lives were far too complicated as it was. Grandad Nelsan raised my mother by himself. She always said he did the best he could, and his one and only obsession regarding her was that she got the best education she could. My mother graduated from Emerson College, and it was Granddad's proudest day; he told her that over and over again too."

"My father's mother—Caroline was her name—I don't know much about her. She left them when my dad—his name was Ryan—was a baby, and she died a few years later. Her people seemed to have disappeared after her death; I've tried to connect, but there seems to be no one left. My parents used to see each other around the farm, though they grew up worlds apart. Somehow, they gravitated to each other: he, the-son of the king of the manner, and she the farmer's daughter."

"Oh, no," Cassandra started. "He didn't force …"

Michael shook his head. "It was true love, yet no fairy tale ending."

"Not Meghan and Harry then."

He shook his head, not laughing this time. "Dad's family—his father—hated the entire situation. He forbade it and threatened to fire Granddad Nelsan to ruin him. Can you believe that madness? So, they tried to keep away from each other. Couldn't. Snuck away and got married. When Grandfather found out about it, he threatened to disinherit my father, his only child, even had the papers drawn up. Yet, my old man didn't give in; he stood his ground, and they stayed together as long as they could."

"What happened?" she asked quietly.

Michael shrugged. "Life. He got sick—lung cancer. Needed money for care and went back to the homestead. My mother understood. She always said, 'If she couldn't live with Ryan, she wouldn't live with anyone else.' They lived apart for many years. She in Roxbury, and despite that, they never divorced. So, when he died, he left me an inheritance he'd doubled, and I tripled to my surprise, and it's more than enough that I can give back.

"She'd be so proud of you, Michael. The clinic's your next project, right?"

He nodded. "Then, if we can bring more affordable housing to the neighborhood, that's number one in need."

"You're actually making your dreams come true."

"You can too."

144

Cassandra's reply was touched with a slight bitterness: "I'm trying."

He put his arm around her shoulders and pulled her close. They sat, enjoying the beauty of the day and, more importantly, the warmth of each other.

***

When Michael pulled up in front of Talia's house, he turned off the car before looking at her. Enclosed in this luxury box with him and his presence overwhelmed Cassandra's mind, put her on lusty edge, was all she could think to call it.

"We're having the opening for the theater soon; a big-deal gala," he said with exaggerated annoyance. "I have to show; so would you like to go with me, that is, if you're still in town? I know it won't be like the parties you're used to. At least it'll be something to do, and I promise it'll be fun."

Cassandra looked at him, his handsome face and dark penetrating eyes. The space his athletic body commanded, the aura of success, wealth, and generosity that surrounded him made him more glamorous than any movie star she'd ever met. Michael was for real, and all this made him overwhelming in a sense. She felt suddenly angry that she was being pulled back in by her family, her hometown, by this man and her overwhelming love for him; forces that made her life in Hollywood seem not thousands of miles away, but millions and so itty-bitty tiny compared to what was here sitting in front of her. She had to force herself to break away.

"I don't know," she said. "I might try and get an earlier flight home. Anyway, I'm here ultimately to evaluate my life, figure out what I think I want is actually what I do want, not to stay around forever."

He nodded. "I understand. You have things to work out, your own projects you're pursuing."

He got out of the car, came around, and opened the door

for her. When she'd gotten out and stood before him, he brushed a kiss across her cheek before saying goodbye.

As she made her way up the stairs to her sister's third-floor apartment, Cassandra took in a deep breath. She could still smell a whiff of his cologne, and sighed; she loved a man who wore great cologne.

When Cassandra walked into her sister's living room, still feeling good, she found Talia slouched in an over-stuffed chair in the semi-darkened room. The television was on, playing *The Wizard of Oz* while Alicia Keys played in the background. Cassandra frowned. Oh no, her sister only listened to Alicia when she was feeling down. "The Color Purple" by Alice Walker sat on her lap.

When Cassandra turned on a lamp, her sister jumped, almost dropping the book.

"Whoa, sorry."

"No, I didn't hear you come in."

Cassandra picked up the remote control and started to press the *off* button, but Judy Garland was singing "Somewhere Over The Rainbow," the version she believed would never be topped, so she listened until Judy was done, then turned off the movie.

"Michael just dropped me off and wanted to pick up my other bag. Can you drive me over to the folks?"

"Yeah, sure," her sister said vaguely, and instead of going back to the book, she stared at the flat, lifeless television screen.

Cassandra sat across from her. "What's the matter, Talia?"

Her face sat in pensive lines. "I introduced Katelyn to Mom at the party, and being Katelyn, she was personable, kind, and funny."

"What did Mom say?" Cassandra asked warily, though she had an idea where this was going. She really didn't want to hear the answer but knew she had no choice.

Talia sighed. "That she seemed nice but was also arrogant and self-absorbed, and she didn't get why I didn't see it. But I see it now."

"You see what Mom wants you to see, but that doesn't mean it's true, Talia. I met Katelyn and didn't pick up on any of it; as a matter of fact, the exact opposite. I found her lovely, just like you said."

Her sister shook her head. "Katelyn is somewhat bossy, Cass. And the few times we went out? I caught onto more negative vibes."

"Talia, you're not going to let Mom's words influence your growing feelings for Katelyn. It's wrong."

"Already done," her sister said with a touch of self-depreciating sadness.

"Mom's words—"

"Matter big time," Talia cut in with a snap as she sat forward, causing her book to fall to the floor. "Especially to the lesbian daughter of a Pentecostal-church-going-member-in-good-standing."

"You shouldn't care so much," Cassandra said softly, feeling her sister's pain. She picked up the book and sat it on the table.

"But I do." Talia's words were just as soft. "I was her one and only for a long time before she married your dad: just us against the world. We were so close—even when you and Layla came along—until the truth came out about me and she saw who I really was, what I am. You two don't have that extra …" She halted thoughtfully. "I don't even know what to call it." Then. "Layer, that's it. What she has to dig through to understand me, let alone accept what she really doesn't want to. I'm the darker sister, after all, literally and figuratively."

"Talia, please." Talia's pain was deep and at this moment, Cassandra had no idea how to handle it. "Mom, loves you."

"With reluctant acceptance, I believe. I know, it's my problem that I want that closeness still and can't have it if I flaunt who I am in her face. But I may not be able to keep important aspects of my life off her periphery, especially now that I'm back to stay."

Cassandra was stunned by her sister's words and the deep anguish surrounding them. She took her sister's small hand and held it in both of hers. "You're who you are: a wonderful, loving, woman. What about your own joy?"

"Who's truly joyful in this world, Cassie? Except for little kids."

"I want you to be happy, and Layla too."

"What about you?"

The question caught Cassandra off guard, with no sudden answer from her forthcoming. At that moment, Talia's phone pinged an incoming message, and seconds later so did Cassandra's. They picked them up, looked at the screens, then at each other.

"Mom," they said in unison.

"She wants us to come over for a family dinner, in the middle of the week," Cassandra said. "When those are usually on Sunday … and big productions."

"Supposedly to celebrate your homecoming, Cass," Talia said. "What're we gonna do?" she sounded fearful.

Cassandra stared at her sister. "Go, of course. We would dare not."

**

When Michael pulled away from dropping Cassie off, he meant to go to the theater and check on how the preparations were coming for the opening night festivities. Instead, he drove until he got to Cambridge Street, where he turned off and headed up I-90. He didn't think about what he was doing, just did it. He drove until he reached the outskirts of Somerset, where his grandfather, whom he hadn't seen in more than a year, lived.

Somerset, at first glance, looked an enchanted English village complete with thatched cottages crawling with ivy and roses encircling mullioned windows. There were cobbled stone streets, a village green, and a small river that ran through it called the River Cambria.

There was a high street complete with tea and chocolate shops, a bookstore, a place that sold handmade scarves and caps, a restaurant pub, and even an old stone church, non-denominational. The place was so idyllic, one expected to see Miss Marple types traipsing down the cobblestones. This bucolic, tranquil, ideal town was created, Michael knew, for those with means; Somerset was a financial haven only for the extremely wealthy, their minimum income around a million a year.

As he drove through the town, he took in how serenely beautiful it was this summer afternoon, with many of its residents in their gardens or talking with their neighbors in front of their cottages, all seeming without a care in the world. His grandfather's home was outside the village but in walking distance, though Michael knew the old man rarely ventured that way; he preferred his own company.

He slowed in front of the small cottage made of rust-colored stone, its front door painted a bright and welcoming yellow. The place looked friendly and inviting, Michael thought, though knew it was only an illusion. The house's interior was as contemporary as money could buy; his grandfather enjoyed his creature comforts way too much to give them up.

Michael parked the car round the side of the house next to a rugged Range Rover. As he exited, the yellow door opened and the man himself stood there, his two golden shepherd collies by his side. He knew there were cameras on the property his grandfather regularly monitored, so he had seen him arrive.

Michael walked through the front gate, took a few steps up the walk, and stopped. Stephen Kelly and Michael Kelly faced each other like gunslingers in an old western.

The old man was seventy-seven years old but didn't look it; he reminded Michael of the actor Brian Cox except he was taller and more gnarled. He stared at this man who'd turned his back on his only son because he'd loved a woman of color. Who would speak first? Should he? Or would they stay at this stalemate the rest of the day? A picture of Cassandra popped into his mind, her words, her touch had prompted him to make this overdue visit, a gesture of tempered forgiveness because it was necessary.

"Hello, Grandda," he said.

"Well, Michael. It's been a long time since you've been this way to check if I was still alive."

"I call and text you when I can."

His grandfather waved a dismissive hand. "It's not the same."

"I'm here now."

"Why?"

Cassandra had been right, even though he and this man were miles apart in so many things—attitudes, tastes, beliefs and in a hundred other ways—this was still his family.

"I wanted to see for myself you were doing okay."

"I'm doing fine."

There was silence between them for a few minutes longer. More than silence, Michael thought; it was a gulf. Was it up to him to cross it first or his grandfather? Yet, if Michael didn't make the first move, where would they be? At a cold-war stalemate? An impasse? He thought himself better than that. He wasn't a quitter; he never gave up on anything that mattered, including trying for some of sort of relationship with this man, his own flesh and blood.

"You have any of that atrocious coffee of yours?"

"I always have coffee, and it's not atrocious." His grandfather's lined face frowned. "So, you wanna come in then?"

"For one cup."

"Could be two," his grandfather countered and stepped back into the house. After only a brief hesitation, Michael followed him inside.

CHAPTER SEVENTEEN

It was almost dinner time when Michael pulled up into the driveway of his friend's large green-painted Victorian in Jamaica Plain. As he made his way up the front walk, with a gift box in hand, the front door opened wide, and a few seconds later, a missile, in the form of a small child on a big wheel, came barreling out across the porch and sailed above the stairs. She hit the sidewalk and slalomed sideways, colliding with Michael's legs.

"Luna, what in the world." He plucked the child off the toy and onto his hip as Demarion appeared on the front porch.

"There she is, and there you are," he said. "Glad you showed up."

"Me too, or she'd be barreling down the street by now." Michael addressed the child, "Listen, sweetie, it's not cool trying to be the next Speed Racer."

The little girl, all of five years old, gazed at him innocently. "What's a Speed Racer, Uncle Michael?"

"Eons before your time, sweetie."

Demarion came down the stairs and picked up the big wheel, giving his daughter an admonishing look. "You know better, Luna. Your ma's gonna be mad."

The child threw an arm around Michael's neck. "But Uncle Michael caught me."

"Pop." A skinny teenager, his hair a big, curly afro, appeared in the doorway. "Mom says dinner's almost ready." He looked at Michael. "Hi, Uncle Mike."

Luna wiggled down out of Michael's grasp, ran up the porch stairs, and launched herself at her brother, who caught her in mid-air and carried her inside.

"Your children have to be part jack rabbit."

Demarion stared at Michael seriously. "Is rabbits supposed to be funny?"

He led the way up the stairs and into the house where great smells wafted. From the outside, the house looked like any other nicely kept Victorian on the street, yet inside was an interior designer's dream. It was an open-plan design, with high ceilings, solar paneled skylights, wide windows, and strategically placed, brightly colored walls that designated each section from the other. On these walls hung innumerable pictures of family and friends.

Demarion led Michael into the large kitchen/dining area connected to a family lounge. The lounge was decked out in child-friendly furniture, soft rugs, a fireplace with a large-screen television mounted over it playing an episode of *Peppa Pig*.

Hannah, Demarion's lovely dark-haired, blue-eyed, and very pregnant wife sat balanced precariously on a stool as she wiped cream off the face of three-year-old Sam. The child looked around at them and grinned through the cream on his face.

"What's he's gotten into?" Demarion laughed.

Sam held his arms out to Michael, who placed down his package before picking up the child.

"Hey, big guy Sam." Michael wiped some of the left-over cream off the child's face and tasted it. "Your famous lemon meringue pie, Hannah."

"One of your favorites," she said.

Hannah planted a kiss on Michael's cheek; Sam mimicked the kiss on Michael's other side, making them all laugh.

"I heard the big wheel going," Hannah said and rubbed at her swollen stomach.

"I think Luna wants to do stunts for a living," Michael said and sat the toddler down.

The child waddled over to the family room, where he picked up a child-sized iPad and began pressing buttons.

"Is that for me?" Hannah gestured at the gift box.

"Because you feed my stomach as well as my heart."

"Ah," Hannah gushed and began unwrapping the present.

"That's a suck-up line," Demarion said. He opened the oven door, put on kitchen mitts, and pulled out a steaming vegetable lasagna. He placed the bubbling casserole in the center of the large, rustic family table, where bread and sweet, fresh butter already waited. "You, sit," he said, pulling out a chair for his wife before calling, "Chester, Luna, dinner."

Hannah finished untying the box and took off the top revealing rows of fancy packed teas.

"Thank you, Michael; just what I needed for a quiet cuppa."

"In about ten years," Demarion added.

Chester and Luna appeared, the little girl headed to the refrigerator. She took out of pitcher of water and poured everyone a glass. Chester picked up Sam and settled him into his high-chair before moving to his own seat. After everyone was settled at the table, Luna gave her own version of "thank you for this food and fam" that made them all grin.

They dug into the meal, laughing and talking between delicious bites. At one point, Michael sat down his fork and sat back, enjoying himself while wondering for the first time if he would make a good family man, and believing he actually would. He'd been so busy these last few years, and with his only family situation in flux, he hadn't let himself dwell on being a husband and father.

Yet, the idea—the need—to have one of his own had

never been so strong as it was now since Cassie had appeared in his life and flipped it on its head. He wanted his own version of love and happiness. The fact that she'd come home and turned him on to these truths was bittersweet.

An hour later, Demarion and Michael sat out back in the Archer's stylish outdoor oasis complete with centered fire-pit and living-room-styled couches. His friend was nursing one of his home-brewed concoctions while Michael sipped on a non-alcoholic beer, which was excruciatingly unsatisfying.

The backyard had started out like any ordinary large space with a house full of children; it became a play yard complete with trampoline, swing set, sandbox, and a treehouse. Beyond these kiddy accoutrements was an additional swath of yard Demarion had turned into a miniature farm with a large vegetable garden that included corn; there was even a miniature greenhouse filled with plants.

"Thanks for the drink." Michael held up the bottle.

"That's not a drink; it's beer-flavored water."

Michael laughed, then sobered as he said, "I saw my grandfather today."

"Really? It's been a while. How's the old buzzard?"

"The same; he'll never change, I know that, but it doesn't mean I can ignore him anymore, Dee. Time is getting away from us both, and somebody needed to make the first move."

"Good for you, my friend."

"Oh, and thanks for dinner."

"Someday soon I hope you'll return the favor, wife and babies included."

"Being a part of your life—of theirs—has made me want more."

They were silent for a few minutes, listening to the night sounds of the quiet neighborhood.

"Is it my family life?" Demarion asked. "Or is your

beautiful Cassandra responsible for this monumental change of heart?"

Michael knew that if he could be totally honest with anyone besides Cassandra, it was Demarion.

"When I'm around her, the possibility for more is as bright as a star. Even with my family background, she gets it. She's a big part of it, but not all. Seeing some of my dreams come true, like the neighborhood clinic underway and the recent connection with my grandfather, after no true contact for far too long for reasons that I need to learn to live with, has helped me see what I've been missing, in spite of what I already have."

"What about trying to live up to both sides of your family—the white side versus the Black? What about that existential tussle?"

"The tussle's over. I'm done trying to satisfy either side, instead I'm going to do what I think is right, and that's it."

Demarion nodded at the certainty in his friend's voice.

Before leaving for home, Michael went back into the house to say goodnight to Hannah, who sat in the family room, a laptop rested on her stomach as she studied the screen.

"That's really up close and personal," he said.

"Yeah, this kid's already talented, can hold a laptop on his head." She smiled and put it aside. "You headed out?"

He nodded. "I wanted to thank you for dinner."

"You're always welcome." Hannah studied him. "You and anyone you chose to bring with you are always welcome."

"Uh-oh." Michael recognized the information-gathering-tone. "What has your husband told you?"

"Nothing, he just mentioned a friend of yours Cassandra Chaletain was in town. She's an actor, is that right?" Michael nodded. "Have you ever mentioned her to me?"

"Maybe in passing."

She shook her head. "No, I would have remembered."

He knew this was true. As well as being a loving wife and

mother, Hannah was a fierce counselor in the city's law department.

"Cassie's here for only a short time."

"Then, don't you think you'd better get in there and give her a reason to stay?"

He stared at her, knowing the truth in his heart while seeing it in his friend's eyes. "It's crazy for me to even contemplate, to see Cassie as anything but a friend; our lives are too different. She's lovely, talented, and terrific—always has been. And I believe for her, Hollywood is where she shines best."

"Your Cassandra does sound great, and if so, Michael, a person like her shines bright anywhere."

CHAPTER EIGHTEEN

That evening, a few seconds before six o'clock, Talia pushed open the front door. "Hello," she called as she walked in followed by Cassandra.

The house was full of the wonderful smells of great cooking, barbecued meat and the warmth of home. It struck Cassandra with chords of taunt nostalgia and homesickness. Her feelings made her wonder, for the first time in a long time, why she had really gone away from here, from all of them.

"Right on time," their mother said, coming in from the kitchen into the dining room carrying big bowls of steaming goodies. "Go wash up, then you, Cassie, get the mac and cheese out of the oven."

Cassandra headed to the kitchen door just as her father was coming through from the other side with his own filled bowls.

"Hey, sweetie."

"Hi, Dad," she said, then in a lowered voice, "What's this about?"

"Emergency dinner," he said mildly. "She got up this morning and announced: 'We need to have a family meal to get things straight.'"

"What things?"

"She didn't say, and I didn't ask. I just did my part by

going to the store for the barbecue."

They heard the back door open and looked that way. Layla stepped through with the children following behind her like little ducklings.

"Hi, Dad," Layla said.

"Paw Paw, I fell today, and I think she"—he hitched a thumb at his sister—"pushed me," Nicholas said as they ran up to their grandfather.

"Na-ha," Lexxie chirped.

"None of that, you two," their grandfather admonished. "Gram's in the dining room; let's go."

The three left the kitchen as Cassandra washed her hands, then freed the mac and cheese from the oven.

"You know why she wants this dinner?" Layla asked, sitting an apple pie down onto the counter.

"Hello to you too, and I don't have a clue what she's up to."

The door opened, and their mother stuck her head inside. "The mac and cheese, Cassie; we're ready to sit down. Wash, Layla."

They did as told without another word.

Once all the food was on the table, they took their assigned seats: Talia next to Cassandra and Nicholas next to her. Layla sat on the other side with Lexxie on her right, on her left was the seat designated for her partner, Alex, now empty. The seats had been assigned since childhood; even the grandchildren had their places. After everyone was seated, they joined hands and bent their heads as their mother gave the benediction.

When she was done, they all raised their heads and looked at her.

"Why a family dinner tonight, Mom?" Cassandra spoke up first.

"For one," her mother began while passing around a bowl of string beans, "you're home for the first time in a long while. Two: Talia's living here again, and Layla has more time now for us and the kids." She sat back as the rest of the food was passed around. "Lastly, and the most important reason for this spontaneous get-together: there's a lot of tension within this family." She held up a "staying hand" as mouths opened to deny. "Don't deny it. I know it; I feel it, and so does your dad. I want to know right now what's going on between you three?"

"It's over with, Mom," Layla said.

"What's this 'it'?" their mother asked."

"It's nothing," Cassandra chimed in.

"That new-old-thing gaslighting?" Mrs. Chaletain narrowed her demanding gaze on her daughters. "It won't work on me, so fess up."

"You came home wanting to be Glenda," Layla suddenly said and pointed at Cassandra, "trying to fix our lives."

"A witch?" Cassandra stared at her.

"Witch," Lexxie chirped up.

"No, no, Cass," her sister instantly softened. "She was good, remember? They thought she could fix everybody's life and she couldn't; it was up to Dorothy and the others to do it themselves." She glanced around the table. "It's up to each of us to fix our own lives; that is, if we're brave enough."

Their mother smiled as the others nodded. "In essence: mind your business until you're asked to help. Everybody got it?"

"Got it," the kids piped up in unison.

Cassandra looked at her sister across the table. "I'm sorry, Layla; your happiness is important to me. I love you. I love both my sisters."

"We love you too," Talia said.

"We do," Layla added.

"Then that's settled; we're all loved," their father said. "Come on, let's eat this good food."

After dinner and cleaning up, the sisters sat in their favorite spots at the kitchen table over cups of green tea.

"Speaking of love," Talia said conversationally. "Where's Michael, Cassie?"

"You're trying to be funny, is that it?" Cassandra jumped on the defensive even as she felt a heated flush rise up her face to her hairline.

"Why don't you text him?" Layla asked. "To see if he'd like to come over for a cup of tea. I saw the way he looked at you: he won't say no." She laughed and was joined by Talia.

"Okay, I've had enough of you both for the night." Cassandra got to her feet and spontaneously hugged each sister in turn. "I'll see you two tomorrow; I'm turning in."

"Maybe …" Talia called as her sister exited through the kitchen door.

"You might be busy," Cassandra heard Layla say from the other room as the two women giggled.

Cassandra ignored them, sat down on the hall stairs, and took out her phone, impatient to speak with Michael, heck, to do more than speak with him. As she looked at the screen, it lit up, and she recognized his number.

"I'm coming down your parents' street right now."

"Yes," Cassandra said, and hurried out onto the porch.

As soon as he pulled up in front of the house, she was at the car, pulling the passenger door open and settling inside before he could get out and open it for her.

"I'm in." She slammed the door. "Tell me."

"You were right, my grand—" Michael began excitedly then looked past her. "Your sisters are at the window, staring at us."

Cassandra turned and looked toward the house; her sisters stood at the front door waving at her.

"Let's get out of here before they start taking pictures."

Would you like to go to my house?"

"Boston, Sarasota, or Manchester?" She grinned at him.

"You choose?" he said, not grinning back.

The smile left her face as they stared at each other, both feeling the weight of the question and how the answer would decide their fate … at least for one night.

"Manchester by the Sea," she said quietly.

Michael nodded and, turning from her, started the car and drove them away from the house. Along the way, they hardly spoke, though he took her hand and held it all the while.

When they pulled around the circular driveway and Michael stopped the car at the bottom of the stairs, Cassandra sat a moment, looking up at the magnificent house. It was a glass castle throwing out clean, mellow light from every other window; the warm glow seconded only by the light of the full moon overhead.

Michael opened the car door for her, and she got out. Instead of going up the steps to the house, Cassandra turned toward the sea, which was only steps away down a wide green lawn. The ocean was an endless expanse, the moonlight sparkling off it as if by magic. The waves gently lapped at the rocks below, the sound calm and soothing.

"It's magnificent." Cassandra turned to Michael.

He held out a hand. "Come see the house."

"Let's go down by the water first."

They walked across the lawn and down to a set of rocks above the water, hand in hand. The ocean was a dark, flat, never-ending sheet. Cassandra could see the outlines of islands, but it was too dark to make them out. They stood listening to the waves lap at the rocks, the sound of animals somewhere in the trees along with a slight wind that rustled the leaves. Michael put his arms around her from behind, and Cassandra rested back against his strong chest. They stayed that way for some time, enjoying the moment.

After a while, she took his hand and walked back to the house. Michael led her up the front stairs through a door he must have triggered somehow and into a wide, white foyer, lit by a chandelier overhead. He started to turn toward a room to his left, but she led him toward the wide, sweeping staircase in the center of the mansion's hall.

"Show me the upstairs first."

He led her up the stairs and down a hall to the door on his right, which he opened. He stepped through, leading her inside. The room was large and minimally furnished, with a chest of drawers, a fireplace with a flat-screen television over it, a couch and table, and a huge bed with a tall, dark blue headboard shaped like a wave connected to bedside tables. But what caught Cassandra's breath was the wall of glass that looked out over the ocean. She helplessly walked toward it.

"It's beautiful," she said and stared at the world of water below.

"You're beautiful," Michael said from behind her, and she turned to face him. "Having you here is better than any dream or fantasy I could ever imagine."

She nodded, unable to speak for once in her life. Without any more words, they went into each other's arms.

Their hunger for each other was so great that hands overrode hands as they stripped each other of clothing and kissed as much naked skin as their lips could reach.

The view from Michael's window was spectacular, yet it took second place to his body, which was not overly muscular, yet pronounced and silky smooth. He was beautifully shaped, and it stirred her to a rush, a literal heat; she felt a frisson of it across her forehead, through her body, and especially between her legs; she was melting. Whew! Cassandra literally fanned herself from her steamy desire for him with one hand before putting the other around his erection. It was large, solid, and wonderfully erect; ready for her—their—pleasure. His hands knew how to handle her with the correct amount of strength and passion; it made her near woozy with her own readiness.

"Condom," she managed to breathe out.

"Yes."

He went quickly to one of the tables, pulled open a drawer, and removed a packet. He walked back, opening the packet with his teeth and tossing the wrapper over his shoulder as he handed the condom to her. Cassandra, with shaking hands, rolled it on him as he gave a satisfied sigh.

He took her chin in his hand and kissed her so thoroughly, his tongue playing with hers as her hands pulled him deeply into her. He let her take in a quick breath, then was back for more. He filled Cassandra's senses, and there was only one thought in her mind: Why hadn't she known he was like this? She should have known that it would be a bond fire between them.

Michael turned her, and Cassandra put both hands against the glass wall, catching a moonlight glimpse of her own reflection as he gripped her hips, his fingers firm. He used one leg to spread hers, the fingers on one hand gave her right butt cheek a squeeze before his other hand slipped around and parted her wet lips, feeling her wetness and readiness with gentle fingers.

Cassandra's body reacted with a jolt, her mouth with a moan of pure pleasure. His hands went up to her breast, and he gently squeezed as he kissed the side of her neck before his hands went back to grip her hips as he bent her forward and thrust into her in one swift, decisive move that made them both moan and take in air for two, three, exquisite seconds. They let it out in a rush as they felt each other and marveled at that slippery, soft, hard feel. Then helpless not to, the feel of her was so exquisite, it drove Michael forward—literally.

"Michael, ah, ha," Cassandra shouted as one of his hands went to her right breast and the other tightened on her hip.

Her hands pressed against the glass hard as her legs widened to take more of him in. His thrusts intensified, and she felt the orgasmic wave build inside her, build at his thrusts until it crashed into her, and she screamed. She couldn't help it; never had she felt such a ripple of pleasure.

"Cassandra darlin', hold on," Michael whooshed into her ear.

He pounded hard again, then once more, sending her into another orgasm as his own powerful release sent him over the edge. Her legs buckled, and she would have hit the floor if he wasn't holding her as they sank to the carpet. They lay against each other, breathing through their mouths.

Cassandra was the first to speak. "Well, if I'd known that in high school."

Laughing, Michael stood and effortlessly picked her up in his arms and deposited her on the bed.

"Right back," he said, and headed for the bathroom.

She heard water running for a moment, then he was back with a soft, damp towel, which he ran across her skin, cooling her off. He then pulled the duvet up from the foot of the bed and wrapped them in it. They looked into each other's eyes, gray mesmerized by hazel. Their hands roved over the now-familiar contours of the other's body. Michael's finger traced across her lips. Cassandra ran a hand over his beard.

"It's really soft," she whispered.

"Thank my barber."

She was amazed at his humbleness, how he still had that self-depreciating streak, even after his good fortune.

"You're such a sweet man."

"Since I'm such a sweet man, do you want to go to the gala with me? I figure this is a good time to ask."

Cassandra chuckled. "Probably the best timing ever, and I would love to."

They kissed long and languidly. His hands ran through the fullness of her hair, cupped her generous breast as his lips slid from hers and down the side of her neck, making her skin shiver in renewed anticipation of what was coming next.

"We can go easy and slow," Michael said, taking a nipple into his mouth before his lips made their way down her stomach and beyond. "Take our time."

"All the time in the world," Cassandra said on a shuttering breath as his lips reached the slick welcome between her legs, and she was lost.

It was a few minutes before sunrise when Cassandra slowly awoke wrapped in Michael's arms; the heat of him at her back. She looked out the glass wall and saw the world beyond beginning to brighten. She disentangled herself from the still solidly sleeping man, smiling a little to herself. *He deserves a restful sleep*, she thought, amused, after the wildly active night they'd had.

Pulling on a sweatshirt she found on the couch and taking a blanket off the end of the bed, Cassandra quietly left the room. She left the house through a side door, leaving her curiosity over the rest of the mansion until later, and walked across the lawn down to the sandy beach.

She took a mat off a beach chair and settled herself on the sand, throwing the blanket around herself as she watched the day form, the sun rising over the ocean. A light breeze and bird-song accompanied the relentless lapping of the waves.

Though she felt pleasantly achy and physically spent after her night with Michael, her soul was energized, and she again felt at peace. She believed it was because of a combination of everything: being back in with her family, being recognized for her writing, and, of course, being with Michael had been wonderful.

He was amazing; all this was amazing. It was really too much, wasn't it? Yet, it shouldn't be. She'd met many people—men—out in Hollywood who were more glamorous, had just as much to offer, seemed to have it all, but she hadn't felt a thing for them, and with Michael, it was different, much different, and for this reason she felt a zing of fear she didn't want to contemplate. *Stop this soul-searching*, she told herself, *and just enjoy their time together*, because it wouldn't last forever.

***

Michael woke suddenly, feeling bereft, and reached for Cassandra, only to find her side of the bed empty. He sat up. Where had she gone? He got out of bed, went to his closet, found a pair of jogging pants and a T-shirt he quickly donned before heading downstairs. He saw that one of the side doors was open, and exited. He stood at the top of the stairs where he caught sight of Cassandra sitting on the beach by the water's edge. A feeling of serenity overcame him because she looked like she belonged.

He walked down to her. "Hey," he said and sat down.

"Hey back," Cassandra said. "Want some of the blanket?"

She wrapped it around them both and rested her head on his shoulder.

"It's beautiful here."

"And often times busy. Later on, this afternoon, that waterway"—he pointed at the wide expanse—"will be teaming with sail boats, paddle boarders, and jet skis. You can sit for hours watching the traffic."

"Sounds interesting."

"Speaking of interesting, how about breakfast? You have to be starving by now."

"Sounds good," she said, though they made no move to leave the beach.

As the sun rose higher, its warmth started to generate heat, yet neither wanted to go inside just yet. Their closeness felt to both not only a physical thing but even spiritual. They didn't want to give it up just yet. So, they sat a while longer before Cassandra's curiosity about the rest of the place got the better of her.

"Okay, come on; show me around."

"Absolutely, we can start at the boathouse ..." Then after a short hesitation. "I know it's too much. My father left it to me, and I'm not sure if it's a legacy I should keep or give away on principle. "

"Why should you?" Cassandra said, her usual down-to-earth self-getting to the heart of it. "He left it to you. Enjoy it. Let's go to the boat house."

***

They walked down a short walkway to a deep-water boat dock that had attached a long ramp out over the ocean. They took stone stairs up to a tea house that overlooked the water. Michael showed her a set of three patios on different sides of the house, one sat on gray flagstone and featured comfortable loungers that took in the view. There was even an outdoor swimming pool.

When they were finally headed back into the house, Michael asked, "Did you get a chance to meet Demarion when we were at the theater?"

"Yeah, I did; he told me about the zinnias."

"Would you like to go to dinner at his house tonight?"

"I wouldn't want to break in on his family. I'm a stranger."

"They're my family too, and you'll be with me."

"I don't know," she said, hesitating because it felt as if she was getting in way too deep. But, then again, wasn't she already deep in, truly deep, after making love with Michael? That was the ultimate step for her; something she had never done lightly. So, how much further was she willing to go? Meeting his family shouldn't be a big deal, should it? But then, would she see how much she loved him on her face? She felt as if it shown like a beacon.

"Sure, sounds like fun."

"Good."

Inside the house, he gave her a quick tour that included a large workroom, a decked-out gym, a library, and an indoor swimming pool for cool days.

In the kitchen, after a breakfast of toast and scrambled eggs with tomatoes, Cassandra said, "The meal was first class, the tour of the house was lovely, your company gracious, and your body to die for, and I thank you for all of it. But now it's time for me to get home and recalibrate."

"Here's to recalibrating." He kissed her. "Are your parents going to give you trouble for disappearing."

"No." She thought it over for a few seconds then. "They think I'm at Talia's for the night anyway, and she'll take care of it."

They were on their way upstairs when he asked, "Would you have a problem telling them you were with me?"

She stopped on the landing. "For one: I don't have to tell them anything, and for another, most importantly, I need to think about you, me, us ... We really moved fast."

"Yes, we did." Michael nodded. "But with you, it was worth it. We've been on a path toward each other since we were teenagers, Cassie—it was round-about definitely—"

"Way round." Cassandra nodded her agreement.

"Even if you don't think or believe we were meant to be together, I believe it," he said with supreme confidence, his gaze never wavering from her face. "More than I believe in anything else in my life."

"There's other dreams to believe in too, Michael," Cassandra said. It was on the top of her tongue to confess out loud, in the light of day how much he meant to her. But then what? Change their lives, their plans; not realistic and not so easy. She turned from his gaze to make her way toward the bedroom.

CHAPTER NINETEEN

Michael dropped Cassandra off at Talia's house. Talia in turn dropped her off at her parents' place before heading to work. To Cassandra's relief, her parents were out. After a long shower, Cassandra took a nap, and when she woke, decided to take a run. She worked out regularly at home—had to—and her body missed the exercise.

After donning a gray track suit and running sneakers, she left the house through the back door. She ran up the street at an even, steady pace, and as her breathing smoothed out and her mind picked up the steady rhythm, her thoughts went directly to them.

She and Michael had different wants and needs, and she saw no way they could come together to stay together—even if it was something they both wanted.

"Is that you, Cassandra?" a quavering but still strong voice asked, breaking into her reverie.

She slowed and looked around at an older African American woman who sat on a porch, a couple of houses down, a stack of mail and magazines on her lap.

"I thought that was you, " she said in her elderly but steady voice. "That golden hair of yours is a complete giveaway."

"It's nice to see you, Mrs. Blackstone," Cassandra said politely, surprised at finding herself close to the woman's house. She'd been thinking so deeply, she hadn't realized how far she'd run.

Mrs. Blackstone had been a resident on the street since before Cassandra was born. She had seven grown children, a couple whom Cassandra had played with as a kid. No one had ever seen Mr. Blackstone.

"How's your family?" The woman gestured Cassandra nearer." Come on up, my hearing isn't what it used to be."

With some reluctance, Cassandra made her way up the porch steps. "How's everyone doing, Mrs. Blackstone?" she asked in turn.

The woman waved a dismissive hand at her. "Alive and well. Did you know I have a total of fourteen grandchildren and counting; Jamala's due a baby girl in November."

"Congratulations," Cassandra said, meaning it. "Jamala will make a great mother."

Mrs. Blackstone's still sharp gaze narrowed on Cassandra's ringless hands. "So, what about you? When are you going to bring some babies into this world?"

Cassandra kept a straight face. "No current plans for that, Mrs. Blackstone."

"No prospects in the husband department, ha?" She reared back, her eyes taking the Cassandra all in. "I don't believe it."

Not wanting for a second to have her love life and future dissected by her parents' neighbor, whom she hadn't seen in years, Cassandra started jogging in place.

"I have to get on with my run now, Mrs. Blackstone. It was nice to see you."

Cassandra started down the porch steps as Mrs. Blackstone got up from her chair and came to the porch's edge calling after her, "Tell your folks I said hello."

"I will."

Mrs. Blackstone came down the walk as Cassandra ran up the street. "Time is not promised to us, young lady," she practically yelled, "so you got to make the most of what you're given before it's too late."

"Yes, Mrs. Blackstone," Cassandra called back

Instead of running home, she walked back there slowly, her thoughts jumbled. What had Mrs. Blackstone been talking about? Too late for life, for love, and happiness? It was that time thing again. Should she toss away what she'd worked and strived for all these years for love? She couldn't. She was not a quitter and wouldn't give up on her dreams. So, what was she going to do?

***

Michael went home to his Boston apartment, showered, and dressed, then went over to the theater, where the preparations were underway for the night's event. Everybody in Roxbury had been invited along with Boson-proper notables and even a few of the Boston famous.

In the restaurant's kitchen, he talked to Gaspard and watched for a while as he and his team prepared for the feast that would be part of the event; though his mind was really elsewhere, on Cassandra and the night and morning they'd spent together. After a while, he retreated outside and stood at the green and growing space Demarion had cultivated.

Small green shoots were already rising from the rich earth; new life was happening right now. Things were becoming, changing, growing, and what was he doing? He paced in front of the green. *How odd*, he thought. He'd never felt this bereft before, and the problem was that he knew exactly why. It was because Cassandra was leaving soon. Where would that leave him?

Here in Boston was where he belonged, of course. But the thought of not having Cassandra here every day was … unbearable. But what was he going to do about it? He was going to ask her to stay; he had no choice. Love. Dammit.

***

In the late afternoon, Michael picked Cassandra up and

they drove over to Demarion's house. As he parked in front of the beautiful Victorian and they got out, they heard screams and high voices coming from the back of the house.

Cassandra looked at Michael. "You sure a sports team doesn't live here?"

"No, but a wild family does."

"Then I can't wait to meet them."

Instead of going up to the front door, they followed the noise around back, where they found what did look like a sports team. There were six adults and eight children of various ages, with two of the adults—Cassandra recognized Demarion in the fray—playing a raucous game of soccer. Everyone was so involved in the game, they didn't notice Cassandra and Michael as they approached until a heavily pregnant women with a cute toddler on her hip turned their way.

"Michael," she said.

The baby held out his arms to Michael, who took him and blew raspberries under his neck, making the baby giggle in delight.

"Hi, Hannah, you guys invited the neighborhood to dinner, I see." He turned to the woman standing beside her, who waved. "Hey, Tierra."

"No," Hannah said, her gaze on Cassandra. "It's Tina and Bobby coming to get their kids while Tierra is taking ours."

Michael turned to Cassandra. "Hannah, this is Cassandra Chaletain." He kissed the baby's cheek. "This big boy is Sam."

Baby Sam looked at Cassandra, then held his arms out to her. Cassandra easily took the baby, who snuggled up to her chest and closed his eyes.

"I've never seen him do that before," Hannah said, staring at Cassandra in amazement. "Have you, Tierra?"

"Never," Tierra said.

"I'm slathered in kid smell from my niece and nephew, that's why," Cassandra said, "he couldn't help himself."

The two women burst out laughing.

"Slathered in kid smell," Tierra repeated, chuckling some more. "I'm going to use that the first chance I get."

Cassandra gently patted the baby's back, a natural motion she'd done for Lexxie and Nicholas.

One of the men on the sidelines whistled through his fingers and stopped the game generating a chorus of, "We won," and high-fives from the older children.

"It's time for you all to get going," Demarion called. "We're done being humiliated by you raga-muffins."

"Don't forget your backpacks," Hannah called.

"Here, I'll take him," Tierra said and took a sleepy Sam from Cassandra's arms. "He'll nap all the way to our house."

It seemed as if the yard and the house emptied of all folks under eighteen, along with the other adults in mere seconds, leaving only Cassandra, Michael, and the Ashers to enjoy the quiet. They sat out back drinking sweet tea and chatting amicably.

"We were going to barbecue out," Demarion said, "but it's way too hot."

"Boston's heat is like no other," Cassandra said. "It's the thick humidity."

"You live in L.A., right?"

Cassandra nodded. "It's a different kind of heat, maybe because it's the Pacific winds that help."

"Not to mention the earthquakes and forest fires that blow through," Demarion said.

"And for your neck of the woods," Cassandra shot back. "Nor-Easters and the polar-vortex."

Hannah laughed. "She's got you there, my smart aleck husband."

"She did, and because winter's always around the corner here, that new snowblower I told you about, Michael? It came in yesterday," his friend said. "It's amazing, wanna see it?"

"Do I have any choice, Dee," Michael said drily.

Hannah stood—it took her a few seconds to get there—

and began gathering up the half-empty tea pitcher and the tray. Cassandra jumped up and gathered the used glasses.

"Let me help," she said and followed Hannah into the house, which smelled of baking chicken. "One time when my sister Layla was pregnant—she was only pregnant twice—she was holding a set of china dinner plates and the kid kicked her hard from the inside, walloped her so good, that she dropped the entire stack of plates right onto a marble floor."

"The sound of that must have been awful," Hannah said and placed the things on the kitchen's island counter. "How long have you lived in California? Which movie stars have you met? Do you have anyone special back home?"

"A few down-to-earth movie stars," Cassandra said, taken aback by the rush of questions, especially the last one. She put the glasses into the sink and answered the other two, "Fourteen years and, no, I don't."

"Good," Hannah said and turned off the oven before opening the door and peering inside.

Cassandra wondered which question had prompted the "good." She looked around the warm, bright kitchen-cum-family room, where toys sat neatly stacked in a corner. Story books lay on a table; she picked one up—*Mae Among The Stars* by Roda Ahmed—and ran her hand over the bright cover; she'd read this one to Lexxie and Nicholas.

In one corner were stacks of pampers and packages of baby wipes ready for the new baby's arrival. *This house is without a doubt, a home—one filled with a lot of love and life*, Cassandra thought, even as she felt a stab of envy at what the Ashers had created.

She glanced out the entry doors and saw Michael and Demarion walking back toward the house, Michael was laughing at something his friend was saying. What if Michael was walking toward their home, where their family waited? Did she dare imagine it? Yes, of course she could; she had a good imagination.

When the two men entered the kitchen, Hannah said,

"I'm hungry," and rubbed her belly. "Rafael's hungry too. What about you all?"

"It smells delicious," Cassandra said. "Can we eat outside? It's turned into a gorgeous evening."

"Al fresco." Demarion grinned.

**

They all helped get dinner onto the patio table under a string of soft lights. The meal consisted of chicken piccata, a green salad, fresh asparagus, and home-made rolls. They ate, talked, and drank more sweet tea under the cool night. Cassandra couldn't remember the last time she'd enjoyed being with another couple so much.

"Michael, could you help me get dessert?" Hannah asked. "It's a couple of bowls."

"Of course," he said and went around the table to help Hannah to her feet.

"I really like her," Hannah said, spooning small sponge cakes into a bowl and covering them with fruit then a small dollop of rich cream from a bowl sitting on the counter. "She's good for you."

"She's going back to L.A. soon."

"Children like her," Hannah stated as she placed the dessert bowls and spoons onto a tray.

Michael stared at her. "What does that mean?"

"Well, children—especially babies—can sense if a person's good or bad."

"Hannah …" Michael began. "That's—"

"No, look it up," she interrupted him. "A study conducted at Yale proved it's a fact." She stared at him with total seriousness. "I know that may not pull much weight with you, but what should is that you've been alone for far too long and life is desperately short. If a chance at true love presents itself—a rare and precious thing in itself—don't dismiss it or turn it away because you're afraid."

"There's nothing I'm afraid of."

"Love," Hannah said, "and who came blame you when you haven't had much of it in your life and what you had, is gone. And when she's gone ..."

Michael moved over to the window and looked out at Cassandra, who sat in animated conversation with Dee. The moonlight shone on her, radiating the warmth, originality, and sweetness everyone felt when around her, especially him. Hannah was right; he'd even figured it out for himself: his days without Cassandra would be as cold and bleak and lifeless as a day in Boston in deep winter. His love for her, he knew it now, was deep to the marrow.

***

After dessert had been eaten, they all helped with the clean-up then sat talking a while longer until Hannah, with both hands over her mouth, yawned hugely.

Michael got to his feet. "Time for us to go and you to get some rest."

"Michael's right," Cassandra said, standing too. "Thank you both for inviting me into your home and for a great meal and your especially nice company."

"We'll see you soon?" Hannah asked Cassandra as she and her husband walked them to the front door.

"I hope so," Cassandra said, and on impulse, gave Hannah a hug. "Good night."

"Good night, you two," Demarion said.

They left with the Ashers watching them into the car and down the street. When they arrived in front of Cassandra's house, Michael parked. "I can't wait to see you again at the party tomorrow."

"Then kiss me goodnight, so tomorrow can get here fast."

Michael kissed her deeply, tongues entwining, lingering over it, both wanting more and for tomorrow to hurry up and get there.

It took Cassandra most of the next day to find the right dress since she hadn't brought a serious party frock with her. Yet, it only took her an extra thirty-five minutes to get ready for the gala, and that was all due to the dress itself. She'd found the frock at Diane's, a small, popular boutique in Hyde Park. It was strapless, form-fitting, and the color of champagne. It made her skin, delicately tanned by the sun, gleam, and her hair with it streaks of sun-made gold shine. She put on only light makeup and lighter rose-touched lipstick and wore no jewelry. Gazing at herself in the mirror, she thought, in this dress, she would even give a starlet at the Met Gala a run for her money.

It took Cassandra and Talia—who looked stylish in a blue suit with a lemon-yellow shirt—more than a quarter of an hour to get to the Roxbury Theater because of all the traffic headed that way. The party was a huge community affair, and it seemed everyone in the community had shown up.

It was easy to see the theater before they got to it; it blazed like a star in the night. Two large klieg lights shone out front, and the marquee read, *Welcome All*, in tall, blazing letters. A red carpet was spread out at the entrance. A profusion of flowers along with gold and black balloons decorated the exterior.

A large crowd of people milled around the front to see and be seen. Near the curb stood a line of valets. When they pulled up, one of the men jumped out to open the door for them while holding out a hand for the car keys, which Talia tossed to him. They walked the red carpet with a group of excited party-goers and entered through the double doors.

The carpet led through the lobby and out through another set of open doors right into a huge glass pavilion that was decked out with two chandeliers, round damask-covered tables set with plate and glassware along with centerpieces of yellow and white roses. There was a dance floor in the middle and a crowded bar each side of the room.

"Whoa," Talia said.

"Whoa, is right," Cassandra agreed.

They stood people watching for a while, admiring the gowns and ensembles that floated around them as more people entered the pavilion.

"Wait a sec," Talia said, unsmiling. "Where's the DJ booth? I'm going to find out where I'm supposed to play—I'll see you later." She walked off.

Cassandra stared around, even waved at a couple of people she recognized from the neighborhood. Not yet seeing who she was looking for, she felt someone lightly touch her arm and turned to find Katelyn at her side.

"Hi, Cassie, nice to see you again."

"You too." Cassandra smiled warmly at her. "You look great."

The young woman looked beautiful in a knee-length, spaghetti-strapped disco dress in shimmering gold she wore with strappy, black high-heeled sandals.

"Thanks, you do too." Katelyn nervously touched her dark hair she'd piled up in ringlets on her head. "I hoped it'll cheer me up." Then, looking toward, the DJ circle, she said, "Talia's getting ready to get it started."

"She'll have everyone up and dancing in record time; no pun intended."

Katelyn smiled briefly. "I've left her a couple of messages, but she hasn't gotten back to me."

"Give her some time," Cassandra said gently.

Katelyn nodded, a shimmer darkening her eyes. "I will, because she's great. And because of you, I can tell her family's great too. Have a good time tonight."

"You too," Cassandra said as the young woman walked away until she was lost in the crow.

Cassandra wasn't psychic, so she had no idea if it would work out for them, and this made her suddenly sad.

CHAPTER TWENTY

"You showed," a booming voice made her jump. She turned and watched Demarion coming toward her, decked out in a white tuxedo and black bow-tie, his arm around a beautifully dressed Hannah, who wore a dark green dress that lushly shaped her full body and complimented her maternal glow. "I told you she'd be here before us."

"You did." Hannah patted his cheek affectionately before she kissed Cassandra's.

"You look terrific, Hannah. And you, Demarion, handsome, handsome."

"Don't I know it, while you're stunning."

"How I like a man who tells nothing but the truth." They laughed, and Cassandra addressed Hannah, "I never asked you when Rafael was due to arrive?"

"Two weeks, which means any time."

"And here comes their proud godfather," Demarion said.

Cassandra felt Michael before she saw him and turned to watch as he walked through the crowd toward them. He was wearing a beautifully cut black tuxedo with pristine white shirt and dark bow tie. There was always something to be said about a man who looked great in just about everything he wore—and didn't wear—she thought.

He stopped in front of her, their eyes going to each

other's mouths as Michael touched her cheek.

"You look great," he said softly.

"So do you," she returned.

They stood, the party going on around them as they concentrated on each other, in a world all their own.

"Hello, Michael," Demarion and Hannah said at the same time.

He glanced around at his two friends, who waved at him.

"You ready for your big night?" Demarion asked.

"It's Roxbury's night more than mine," Michael said. "Hannah, please sit for a while."

"We're all right." She patted her stomach. "My husband is going to take me over to the bar for a ginger ale, while you have people to speak with, Michael, and who want to speak with you."

"My wife's wish is my command," Demarion said. "See you both later."

The two left, Demarion making a path for his wife.

"I should circulate too. Want to go circulating with me?" Michael asked, making Cassandra smile.

"That's the nicest thing you've said to me in the last ten seconds."

As they walked through the large crowd, sometimes holding hands, they were stopped here and there by people eager to talk with Michael. To Cassandra's astonishment, many were famous, like Tom Brady, the renowned NFL quarterback and former New Englander.

At one point, Cassandra clutched Michael's arm in shocked surprise. "I don't believe it," she whispered. "Oh, she's coming this way."

"Who?" Michael looked where she was directing.

"There," she said excitedly. "Here she comes."

"Michael, this is fun," said a small, pretty woman wearing a bright grin.

"Uzo." He smiled warmly at the woman who kissed him on both cheeks. She was wearing an off-the-shoulder, delicate blue dress that made her silky, dark brown skin glow. "I'm glad you could make it."

"I wouldn't have missed this for two Oscars, Michael," the actor Uzo Aduba said with a laugh. "What you're doing for Roxbury is outstanding, and I'm happy to contribute to its greatness."

Michael turned to Cassie. "This is Cassandra Chaletain."

Cassandra immediately felt tongue-tied at meeting someone whose work she'd admired for so long. Recovering quickly, she said, "It's a pleasure and honor to meet you, Ms. Aduba."

"Uzo, please."

"Jackie Elliott keeps a picture of you on center stage during class. She points to it and tells us: 'She's celebrated, and you can do it too if you keep at it.'

Uzo smiled. "I studied with Jackie all the time when I was in L.A. I knew it, just by looking at you, that you're an actor too. I'm doing a play in New York for the rest of the summer and will be back on the West Coast at the end of the season. Maybe we can get together for coffee, Cassandra. Or better yet"—she grinned—"pie. Michael'll give you my number."

She kissed Michael on both cheeks once again. "I'll leave you two to enjoy yourselves. I just spotted Conan O'Brien across the way, and he owes me time on his podcast."

She moved off, a small bundle of energy arching through the room, ignoring those who recognized her and stared. When she reached Conan, they embraced in greeting.

Michael took Cassandra's hand. "Come on, I have something to show you. Well, some place."

"Is it going to be a cozy affair?" she asked playfully.

"You'll see."

He led her out of the pavilion and into the theater proper, where he opened a door onto a storage room full of boxes.

"So far not so cozy," Cassandra acknowledged.

"It's worth the circuitous route," Michael said.

He led her around stacked boxes and through a narrow

door that opened onto a set of narrower stairs they climbed up. At the top, Michael flicked a light switch on the wall.

"Cool," Cassandra said as the colored light bulbs strung along the ceiling illuminated the room. "This is like that movie with Julia Roberts; though I hope this doesn't end in shots fired."

"I promise you it won't. So, check it out."

The room was filled with stacks and stacks, shoulder-high, of all sorts of costumes: dresses, shoes, hats, pants, shirts, jewelry; everything anyone could want to play dress-up.

Cassandra eagerly pulled out from a stack a dress that reminded her of the one Glenda wore in the *Wizard of Oz*: sea green tulle and awash in sparkles. She put it against herself and sashayed back and forth. "Nice, ha?"

"Beautiful," Michael said quietly.

He wrapped his hands in Cassandra's hair as he planted a kiss on her lips, then down the side of her neck, making her shiver.

"I'm hot." She stepped back and, staring into his gray eyes, dropped the Glenda dress, then pulled down the side zipper on her own.

Staring into her hazel gaze, Michael removed his jacket and tie. Cassandra slid the dress down her body, reveling a flesh-colored thong and a companion strapless bra, both hugged her shapely curves to distraction. Michael lifted Cassandra out of the dress, and when she was settled onto the floor, her hands undid the button and zipper on his pants before tunneling around the waistband and pushing them and his underwear down his legs.

Their mouths locked as Michael, in two swift motions, removed her bra and underwear. Pulling back, he took a condom from his pants pocket, ripped it open, and placed it on his ready erection before he went back in for another passionate kiss. Ready for him, Cassandra gave back as good-as-she-got as he picked her up, causing her to wrap her legs tightly around his waist. He settled her back against a tall stack of blankets and rugs.

"The feel of you is beyond amazing," Michael whispered, staring into her eyes as he placed a finger on her wetness, making her moan helplessly.

He slipped himself into her wetness, and they froze, savoring the intense pleasure of their connection.

"Soft." He pumped once. "Sweet."

Cassandra tightened with the feel of him as she clutched his shoulders, holding on as he moved his hips again.

"Hard," Cassandra said as her rhythm matched his.

For a while, there were no more words, only sounds: harsh breathing, groans of earth-shattering pleasure, sweat-glazed flesh meshing with flesh.

Cassandra thought they were magnificent together before being suffused with a rising, expanding orgasm that hit her like a sonic explosion and made her not shout but wail; it was that sensational. Michael pumped faster and followed her over the edge seconds later with his own shout of completion at the super-heated pleasure.

When they both caught their breaths and he let her legs slide down his body, Cassandra managed, "Promise me one thing?"

"Of course." Michael brushed her damp hair back off her face.

"The next time, can we make it to a bed?"

He wrapped her in his arms in answer.

CHAPTER TWENTY-ONE

After making themselves presentable again, they left the loft room. They made their way to the lobby, where a few people milled around talking and admiring the lobby's African architecture. They sat down close together on one of the strategically placed loungers that gave the lobby an additional taste of decadence, and took in in the crowd. Feeling languid and satiated, Cassandra rested her head on Michael's shoulder.

"Thank you for tonight," Michael said quietly. "Thank you, for everything."

"You've made a lot of people feel good tonight, including me."

"Hey, are you hungry?" he suddenly asked. "I'm starving. Let's go get something to eat."

"And to drink; I seem to have developed quite a thirst from my recent activities."

They walked hand-in-hand back into the pavilion where a three-tabled-buffet was set up, groaning with food and drink. A young man approached them holding two cellphones.

"Mr. Kiley, are you ready for your speech? We have twenty minutes slated."

"Frank, five minutes—if that—will be more than enough." He turned to Cassandra. "I'll join you in a minute.

Stake us out a table if you can."

The two men moved off as Cassandra moved over to the buffet table. She picked up a plate and stood perusing the large array of food. She was trying to decide between shrimp and salmon when a familiar voice spoke from behind her.

"Cass, my love."

"Langston," she said, putting down the plate and turning to him. "You made it, I am surprised."

Langston, with his wide grin on full display, stood holding the hand of a woman who was his extreme opposite in just about every way. She was at least four inches taller than he was, with dark, blond dreadlocks down to her waist. Her skin was the color of a Brazil nut and darker freckles ran across the bridge of her nose. Her eyes were a piercing chocolate brown above her small, serene smile.

"Cass, you finally get to meet Shauna."

"You're real," Cassandra said.

Shauna laughed. "Definitely."

"I had begun to wonder if you were just a figment of Langston's imagination."

"You see for yourself," her friend beamed proudly. "Alive and gorgeous. You, Cass"—he took her in—"look lovely."

"Why thank you, sir. While I must confess, I'd forgotten how good you look in a suit, Langston."

A sound from the front of the room caught their attention, and they looked that way. Michael was there, a small microphone in his hand.

"Thank you all for coming," he said. "It's terrific to see you all. This theater is your home; you're always welcome here, and I'm honored to let you know that."

There was a loud round of applause, and with a slight bow, Michael left the stage, joining Cassandra and his friends a few moments later. They all partook of the buffet, found a cozy table in a corner, and sat eating and reminiscing, never forgetting to include Shauna in their nostalgic and often hilarious conversation. At one point, Cassandra sat quietly back and basked in the feeling of being loved, accepted, and appreciated; it had been a long time since she'd felt this kind of supreme happiness, if she ever had. Michael's gaze touched her again, as it often had.

A female singer took the stage with her band and began singing in a sweet imitation "Caught Up in the Rapture" by Anita Baker.

"Would you like to dance?" Michael asked.

Cassandra took his hand. "To Anita, of course."

With a number of other couples, they took to the floor. They held each other, swaying more to the now-known-rhythm of each other's body, secure in their own world. For Cassandra, the feeling of Michael's strong body, the knowledge of his kindness, his generosity, made him a wonder to her. Hollywood not only seemed worlds away, but universes.

Lost in his arms, she almost didn't feel her phone ping. She fished it out of her bag thinking it was Talia wondering where she'd gotten off to. It was Marty.

"I'll be back in a second," she said and left the dancefloor, exiting into a miraculously quiet hallway.

"Cassandra, I'm glad I caught you. I have some great news. Are you sitting down?"

"You've been around actors too long time, Marty. Please, just tell me."

"I have something great for you, an audition for the upcoming Jordan Peele production; the part of the assistant in the mental hospital."

"Really? How many lines?"

"You get more than a few lines, Cassandra—you get an entire scene," he announced in joyful anticipation of her appreciation. When she didn't say anything, leaving a silence on the line, he asked, "You still there?"

"I'm still here."

"You have to audition, of course, but you'll ace that with no problem. It's a good start, Cassandra."

Am I still at the start of a career? she wondered silently; one she'd been chasing since she was eighteen years old. "Marty, I'll be thirty years old before I know it, so can't really claim any more starting days."

"Cassandra, you know as well as I do; any new project is a beginning that might take you to the top."

"When is the audition?"

"Monday at one."

"That's tomorrow afternoon, Marty."

"Yes, they wanted to have you here by ten, and I told them you needed time to get back, reacclimate and get into the right space—metaphorically—for the audition."

"Okay," she said, not really listening.

"So, I'll see you by noon tomorrow, then. I'll send a ride for you. Congratulations, Cassandra; I know it's premature, but I know you'll get the part. I'm claiming it for you." He laughed. "Any questions?"

"No, thanks, Marty. Bye." She ended the call and stood there, her mind racing with only one question: what was she going to do?

Cassandra awoke in a light sweat and disoriented, believing it was due to the nightmare she'd had. She'd dreamed she was on a boat out to sea, alone with no other boats or land in sight, except for a fierce storm on the horizon heading toward her. A second later, she realized the sweat on her was because she and Michael were wrapped so tightly together, back to front, skin-to skin underneath the covers that the heat they generated was all-consuming.

Not wanting to wake him, she carefully extricated herself from their entwined limbs, knowing it wouldn't be nearly as easy to untangle him from her heart. She was in love, truly, deeply in love with this man, and she couldn't figure out how it had happened. She'd come home to surprise her parents and, boy, hadn't she been the one surprised. The man lying beside her, had in only a few days, made her realize who she actually was and, more importantly, what she could be.

She got up and stood by the bed watching Michael sleep, while she memorized the lines of his body and the unique handsomeness of his face. After a while, she turned, quickly grabbed her clothes, and went for a quick shower; she needed to leave.

Ten minutes later, she stood in the library staring out the window at Beacon Hill and the golden-domed State house. Yes, she had to leave. All this was too much; it wasn't her world.

Cassandra exited the house through the back door, locking it behind herself, and walked down the street where she caught a cab home. She opened the screen door quietly and entered the kitchen, where she found her mother pouring a cup of coffee.

"Morning, Ma," Cassandra said with a slight wariness she couldn't help.

"Morning back. You want some?"

"Definitely." Cassandra dropped her bag onto a chair and took the proffered cup. She dropped in a teaspoon of sugar as her mother poured herself a cup of the tasty brew.

"You're up early," Cassandra said.

"So are you," her mother shot back. "I picked the garden before your father got up and the sun got too high." She pointed at a row of colanders on the counter filled with more of her garden's abundance.

There was silence between them for almost a minute until Mrs. Chaletain spoke. "You look like you did when you were six and you couldn't decide between which one you'll have for dessert: blueberry or apple pie."

"It's a little more complicated than that. I've been offered a part in a movie, and it's a speaking part … well, almost offered."

"That's great," her mother said, thrilled for her. "Congratulations, Cassie. This is what you've always wanted, isn't it? It's a good thing, right?"

Cassandra tried to sound enthusiastic, thrilled, over the moon. "It is."

"You sound fake, Cassie," her mother said with dead-pan delivery.

"No, Mom; it's what I've been after for so long, and it's now in sight."

Her mother sat her cup down with a thump.

"Then why do you look as if nobody showed up for your first show?"

"I don't; I'm just getting used to the idea, that's all."

"It's him," her mother stated.

"Yes."

"You're in love with Michael Kiley."

Cassandra nodded as tears she couldn't hold back began to fall fast until she was snuffling and her face was a wet mess.

Her mother silently let her go on for a while, then said, "You know I keep myself to myself."

The statement was so boldly untrue, that Cassandra instantly stopped crying and gaped at her until they both helplessly smiled a little.

"That's better." Mrs. Chaletain stood, picked up a tea towel, and gently wiped her daughter's face. "Hear this, Cassie: don't listen to what I say or your sisters or even what your agent says; you listen to your own heart. Now, go get some sleep and decide what you want, what's best for you, and do it."

Cassandra wrapped her arms around her mother's waist as her mother wrapped her back in an embrace that was like no other; it was just pure love. Finally, giving her mother another squeeze, which was almost desperate, Cassandra went to her room. She sat on her bed, looking at the things that hadn't changed much since she was a teenager and thinking, going home again, was definitely not what it was cracked up to be.

***

Michael woke feeling instantly bereft and new immediately why: Cassandra was gone. He got out of bed, found pants, and headed through the house, hoping Cassandra was still there, yet knowing she'd really gone because he didn't feel her. He left the empty house for the garden and paced the cool sandstone tiles.

Pain gripped his heart because not having Cassandra near him actually felt like a physical blow. He was deeply, irrevocably, endlessly in love, and there was nothing he could do about it. Cassandra was determined to have a successful Hollywood career, and she should; she deserved it. She was smart, talented, hardworking, and unstoppable, and that meant he couldn't—wouldn't—stand in her way, no matter how much he loved her.

He stopped pacing, a thought hitting him: if he told her how much he did love and need her, maybe she'd stay. If he gave her a clear choice, staying with him over that empty Hollywood life, she might decide in his favor—their favor. He had to tell her. Hell, what did he have to lose? Nothing compared to what he would gain if she felt the same and stayed.

He heard the phone ring inside and went to answer it. "What's up, Dee?"

"Did you forget the lieutenant governor was stopping by today?" his friend asked immediately. "Her office confirmed this morning. It's no surprise Miss Wilson wanted to meet with you again; she had eyes only for you on her last visit. And, anyway, it gives her reason for another photo op. By the way, the governor sent her regrets for missing last night's party."

"Man, I'd forgotten all about Miss Wilson's stop through today. Can you stand in for me?"

"Nope, I have a meeting with the city council's planning commission along with …"

"All right, I got it." Michael sighed heavily. The last thing he wanted to do was meet with another politician. He needed to find Cassandra and talk; his future was at stake.

"… Speaking of future …"

"What?" Michael asked. He hadn't been listening but that word, already on his mind, got through. "I didn't catch the last part."

"Michael, what's the matter with you?" Frustration laced his friend's words. "You're not tracking here. Lindsey Gerak, the housing chief, will be here too in a couple of hours to go over the plans for the affordable housing complex and green spaces we're developing for the Royal Douglass District. This has been on your calendar for two weeks."

"I know, and it's important, so I'll be there in an hour, but only for the meetings. I have something else I need to do before it's too late."

"What's that?" his friend asked.

"If it works out as I want it to, I'll tell you all about it."

"And if not?"

"If not …" Michael didn't have an answer; all he saw was a blankness.

**

Cassandra had taken her mother's advice. After a long shower, she'd laid down but had been unable to sleep; her mind wouldn't let her. Finally, after twenty minutes of tossing and turning, she'd gotten up and, not knowing what else to do, she picked up the remote and turned on the television for background noise for her thoughts.

The set flashed suddenly on one of her favorite movies *Do The Right Thing*. It was at the scene where Rosie Perez, as Tina, having gotten Spike Lee, a.k.a. Mookie, to visit her by ordering a pizza. Ms. Perez had been new to acting at the time, yet her natural talent and having a role suited to her personality had created one of the most iconic characters in movie history.

"I can try and do that too," Cassandra suddenly said

aloud.

She stood up and paced her room, her thoughts flying feverishly. If she didn't try, she'd never know, and the regret would live with her forever. She took her phone out of her pocket and before she could stop herself, made a plane reservation for Los Angeles. But even with her flight booked, she knew she couldn't leave town without seeing him.

Taking an uber over to the theater, she found him in the theater proper, on the stage watching as additional top-of-the-stage lighting was being installed.

"Nathan." Michael was looking up to the catwalk where the installer worked. "It looks good. Can you install the green and blue lights too?"

Cassandra walked down the aisle and took the stairs up to the stage. Michael looked around at her and smiled as he moved forward, taking her into his arms.

"Katelyn told me you were here," Cassandra said, briefly returning the smile and the hug before she couldn't anymore.

"I was going to call and ask if you'd meet me. I had something important to say to you."

She stepped back away from him. "What is it?"

***

Michael looked at her, the expression on her face was one of sadness and loss. He took her hands and began, "You know I—"

"I'm leaving," she interrupted him, "in a few minutes, back to L.A. Talia's waiting outside to take me to the airport. I was offered a role—at least an audition that sounds positive—but I couldn't go before I saw you."

"I love you, Cassandra." Michael's gray gaze was direct and blazed with feelings for her. "I'm desperately in love with you and will never be with anyone else; I know that like I know time passes. Everything in me, everything I am, wants to tell you to forget about that other world and stay with me and be my love."

"I love you too, so much." A tear slid down her cheek. "I told myself not to cry and be strong."

His hands tightened briefly on hers. "Tell me, and I'll fix it."

Cassandra shook her head. "You can't. Only I can follow my heart and my dreams, and to do both, I have to leave you." She glanced away from his eyes and took in the theater. "A place like this, on a stage, was where I truly realized I was someone—not someone or something unacceptable because I looked too much like one side and not enough like the other. This was the place where what was inside me, the real me, showed up; a stage where I made someone laugh, cry, or think; it's where I mattered, contributed, where I'm whole. If I don't give it another shot. because I'm afraid, I'll never forgive myself."

He looked at her for a long time, then let her hands go. He knew instantly that he was not going to put his wants and needs in a contest up against what she felt was right for herself.

"You're a vibrant, strong, beautiful woman who decides for herself what you want, where your heart will lead you. But know one thing, Cassandra: I'm yours forever." He took the weight of her hair in his hands and pressed her forehead against his. They closed their eyes and remained that way for a few moments longer until he stepped back and let her go.

She turned and left the way she'd come, leaving Michael standing there with his hands ... his life ... empty.

CHAPTER TWENTY-TWO

Talia drove Cassandra to Logan Airport in near silence, neither was in any mood to talk. At the departure gate, they sat in the car, Cassandra staring out at the entrance doors.

"Are you all right?" Talia asked.

"No," Cassandra said, not looking around.

"Well," Talia said slowly, not sure of how to approach the weird situation, "your flight will be leaving soon, and you still have to get checked in."

"Yeah, yeah, you're right," Cassandra said unenthusiastically.

She gathered her two bags and opened her door as Talia got out on the other side to help. Talia found a cart and loaded the bags before she turned to her sister.

"Love you, and I'll miss you so much," Talia said and embraced Cassandra in a tight hug, stifling an attempt at tears. "It's so great when you're around."

"Me too, and I'll miss you too." Cassandra hugged her back tightly. "I hope you and your love works out."

"Me?" Her sister raised eyebrows at her.

"You'd better go before I start blubbering; you can't park long here anyway."

They hugged once more and Cassandra walked into the terminal, unwilling to look back.

***

Michael had watched Cassandra go, watched his future walk away. He'd walked off the stage and stopped halfway up the aisle as Demarion hurried in.

"I've been looking for you everywhere," his friend said excitedly. "I gotta go." He grinned. "Hannah's in labor."

Michael stared at him for a few seconds, then grinned back. "Congratulations to you both. I gotta go, too. I'm leaving for California."

"What?" His friend stared at him, astonished at the news. "When?"

"Right this second because the truth is I'm happiest with her, wherever she is."

"Cassandra," Demarion stated. "I knew it from the start," he crowed.

"I have a plane to catch."

"You're rich, make it a jet," Demarion said.

Michael laughed. "You're right. Kiss Hannah for me, and we'll come back for Rafael's first birthday."

He ran up the aisle with his best friend clapping behind him.

***

Cassandra sat in the business class section, paying no attention as the other passengers boarded. There was only one thought on her mind: what had she done to her life?

She didn't look up, even when the attendant made his announcement. "Ladies and gentlemen, my name is Tommy, and I'm your chief flight attendant on this trip. On behalf of the entire crew, welcome aboard Trans American flight 262, non-stop to Los Angeles. All passengers have boarded and the door is now closing."

Cassandra looked toward the sound of the door whumping shut and the clunk as the attendant secured the latch. She suddenly felt a wave of heat rush over her, sweat popped out on her forehead, and her heartbeat sped up: she needed to get off this plane. This was all wrong. Cassandra unlatched her seatbelt, and before she could move, the pilot's voice came over the speaker, asking everyone to fasten their seatbelt and prepare for takeoff. The plane began to move, and Cassandra realized it was too late.

For the next six hours she vacillated between misery and determination. When she could finally use her phone, she tried making reservations for a flight right back to Boston and couldn't get anything within an hour after they touched down. The earliest plane she could get was a couple hours later, and she booked it. Nothing would stop her from getting back home, back to Michael. On the flight, she tried to call him but got only his voicemail and her text messages got no response.

When the flight finally landed at LAX and Cassandra excited the airport, she stood outside the terminal, just stood there as people moved back and forth around her. She felt the light breeze, the sun on her face and thought the sun was shining in Boston too. Yet she was here while Michael was there. She needed to be wherever he was, like she needed the sun and air. She turned back into the airport. She wasn't going anywhere; she'd wait and be the first on the flight back.

As the automatic doors opened and another group of people rushed out, one of them she instantly shockingly recognized: her Michael.

"Michael." She dropped her bags.

He saw her, pushed around the people between them, picked her up, and kissed her so passionately it made her wrap her arms tightly around his neck, holding on.

When they finally broke apart, he said, "I came because I realized I need to be wherever you are. I have loved you forever and always will. Marry me, Cassie?"

Cassandra hugged him again, tighter, vowing in her heart to never let go. "You're the life I want, Michael. Yes, I'll marry you."

They paid no attention to the people coming and going around them, some who gazed at them wistfully as they recognized true, forever love.

Pulling back for a second, she asked, "But, what about your work in Boston? My work here?"

"As well as being a great background actor; you're a terrific writer, and that can be done anywhere and so can my work. We're great together, and we love each other, meaning we'll work it out."

"I do love you, Michael Kiley, so much, always have." She brushed her lips across his. "And you're right, we'll figure it out, together."

This time their kiss was deep, full of love, and the promise of happiness ever after.

THE END

ABOUT THE AUTHOR

I'm the author of three titles under the name: Lori A Mathews and Lori Ann Mathews. The first two titles contribute to the: *New York City Detective Owen Story* series. The novel titles are: <u>You Don't Know Me</u> and <u>Begin At The End.</u> The series is in the genre of mystery, crime fiction.

My third novel is titled: <u>Our Daughters, Yazhou nu er – The Asian Daughter</u>. It's women's fiction

I love to hear from readers at: loriannmathewsnovels.weebly.com.

.